WildFire

Lynn James

Bella
BOOKS
2011

Bella Books, Inc.
P.O. Box 10543
Tallahassee, FL 32302

Printed in the United States of America on acid-free paper.

First Edition Bella Books 2011

Editor: Karin Kallmaker
Cover Design by: Linda Callaghan

ISBN-13: 978-1-59493-191-8

About the Author

Lynn James lives in Central Oklahoma with her partner of seven years, their teen daughter and spoiled rotten dog. With degrees in English Literature and Engineering, she works in the recycling industry among those dedicated to preserving our planet. *Wildfire* is her first novel.

Dedication

For my partner and daughter who give everything meaning. I love you both.

Acknowledgements

For creative purposes, Captain Elaine Thomas is a composite derived from the numerous positions held by the various members of the U.S. Forest Service. Her character is meant to honor their enormous burden as conservators and protectors of our environment. I thank you all for your service, heroism and dedication.

Robin, my loving, supportive, argumentative and often infuriating partner, thank you for helping make my dreams come true. Our daughter, Angela, who never ceases to amaze me, surprise me and make me laugh. You continue to inspire me and I couldn't be more proud. To my sister, Patty, who survived brain surgery with dignity, poise and humor and my nephew, Trevor, who is proof that there are still amazing young men in the world. You are my heroes and I love you both. Dee Dee and Hauckie, your faith, love and belief in me, helped bring this to fruition. I can't forget my favorite English professor, Susan Spencer, who gave me the confidence to find my voice. Congratulations to Gwen Monarch; you're in a lesbian novel! Thanks to my Mom and Papa David for always being there. I am so incredibly grateful to Bella Books for giving me this amazing opportunity and Karin Kallmaker whose efforts went above and beyond. Your advice, support and attention to detail were more than I could have asked for and there are no words to adequately express my appreciation.

Chapter 1

"I've killed her!"

Stacey wrapped her arms tighter around Devon and let her cry. There was nothing else that she could do.

"Oh God, Stace, she's dead and I've killed her!"

"Dev, honey, look at me." Stacey placed a finger under Devon's chin and tilted her head up until their eyes met, "It wasn't your fault. Ivy is notoriously difficult."

"That's easy for you to say. You aren't a botanist! And ivy is one of the easiest plants to care for!"

Devon McKinney glanced at her watch and sighed as she tried to overcome her frustration at running late. If she just hadn't spent so much time crying over her plant this morning she would be right on schedule.

Her sister, Raine, thought it was silly and although she could count on Raine to be there for her, it was always Stacey she turned to in these situations. Stacey had become accustomed to it. Hell, even Devon herself had come to expect it. They had been best friends far too many years for Devon's sadness over the death of her plant to surprise Stacey. After all these years, Devon was still devastated. Her plants were more than just decoration or a way to spruce up a barren space in a corner. For her, unlike most people, her plants were like pets. She loved them, named them, cared for them and when she lost one, she felt the loss deeply. She couldn't just toss the withered ivy into the rubbish and move on. Instead, the incident had dominated most of her morning, forcing her to get a much later start than she had planned.

Luckily, as usual, there hadn't been much traffic coming out of Barrington. Barrington was a small town on the outskirts of Marblerock. Truthfully, referring to Barrington as a "town" was generous to say the least. If you blinked, you might miss it altogether. After living in Seattle for so many years while attending the University of Washington, it seemed like the perfect place to get away from the hustle and bustle and all the noises that had kept her awake at night. Fortunately, it was only about sixty miles from her alma mater which wasn't too inconvenient when she needed to give a lecture or attend a conference. Barrington didn't have much to offer in the way of entertainment, retail stores or restaurants, but what it lacked in convenience, it more than made up with comfortable silence and tranquility. Not to mention, Marblerock was only twelve miles north and it had many of the conveniences that Barrington lacked.

Once she made it as far as Marblerock, she completed her journey quickly, making up some of the time she had lost earlier in the day. She would have to hurry if she was going to make it to her campsite before the March daylight faded. She pulled her truck to a stop next to the gate that proudly displayed the brown National Forest Service sign that read, "No Unauthorized Personnel." *Does anyone really pay attention to these signs?* She shook her head, but refused to let her late start darken her mood. It was her own fault and now she would have to double-time it in order to make camp before nightfall.

She lifted the heavy trail pack from the bed of her truck with little effort. Reaching behind the seat she found the laptop case and secured it to the backpack. Her water bottle was in the passenger seat along with her cell phone. Finding both, she clipped them to her belt loops. Before heaving the pack onto her shoulders, she crouched down and tightened the laces on her hiking boots. She snapped the chest and waist straps securely into place and located her field bag filled with all the equipment necessary for her assignment.

Once she had all her gear secured, she adjusted her ball cap comfortably in place and locked the truck doors. She attached her key ring to one of the few belt loops remaining and grabbed her walking stick. With one last glance at her watch and then to the sun still shining brightly between the tree branches, she made her way around the gate and uphill to the trail that would lead to her campsite.

She needed to pack for her next assignment, but instead Elaine Thomas lay across her bed lost in thought. Grace's decision to have an affair with a young intern at the ranger's station had been a great incentive for Elaine to volunteer for this field assignment. She had been taken completely by surprise, although she now realized she shouldn't have been. There were many things about Grace that she hadn't learned until they were well into their three-year relationship. And she didn't think it accidental that those truths regarding Grace's beliefs and core values were revealed gradually or not at all...until now.

Only months before, Grace had divulged that the only reason she worked for the U.S. Forest Service was because of some bizarre clause in her grandfather's will, one requiring her to work for a stipulated length of time before she could receive her inheritance. How she could keep that a secret for three years was beyond Elaine. What had made the secrecy so painful was that Grace knew how dedicated Elaine was to protecting the forest and how seriously she took her job. She felt as if Grace and her father, who was responsible for getting her the position, had made a mockery of the Forest Service and all the other agencies charged with protecting precious lands.

Sighing, she punched the pillow and resumed staring at the ceiling. The beginning of their relationship had been good and there had been a point when Elaine thought she would spend the rest of her life with Grace. It had appeared as though they had the same hopes and dreams and enjoyed many of the same activities. She had no doubt that she had loved Grace, or at least the person Grace had been.

Over time, however, conversation had become strained and was little more than sarcastic quips. It had become evident to her that Grace had tried to make her feel inferior, constantly scrutinizing every move and decision, but when Elaine refused to let her, Grace became bitter. Believing that people didn't spend enough effort trying to save their troubled relationships, Elaine had hoped that the woman she once loved would return; only to find that she never really existed. During the past year, the relationship had deteriorated further, resembling one of roommates rather than lovers. Intimacy, physical or emotional, was nowhere to be found. She found more sexual gratification with inanimate objects than she did with her partner and managed to burn up three vibrators in a matter of months.

She knew it wasn't just that they had grown apart; it wasn't a simple communication issue or some other surmountable problem. She found that not only did she not have anything in common with Grace, but that she didn't even respect her any longer. Yes. She had loved Grace, or at least who Grace had pretended to be, but those feelings had changed. Grace's words and actions toward her had revealed her to be a master manipulator.

She sat up, gave the pillow another good punch, then sprawled out again. She couldn't remember the last time she had been truly happy. Which made it all the more ironic that while she had been evaluating her own happiness in the relationship, Grace had been having an affair. She had already decided that something had to change and Grace's actions made that decision relatively easy for her. It was over, she was sure of that. She couldn't abide cheaters and liars and Grace was clearly both.

It would do her some good, she thought, getting away from everyone. It wasn't that she was devastatingly heartbroken over her relationship ending. Hell, she had been contemplating their compatibility and her feelings toward Grace for some time. It was more about her feelings of anger, humiliation and foolishness. She was angry at her so-called friends at the station who knew that Grace had been cheating and had done nothing to clue her in. Some of them had even gone out of their way to help Grace keep it a secret, supporting her deception and betraying Elaine in the process. And nobody, regardless of the state of their relationship likes to be cheated on, especially when they are the last to know.

Yes, she was glad that she volunteered for this assignment. Not that she really had to volunteer. Now that she was one of the few single people in her ranger station, nobody argued when she offered to take the assignment. Few would have dared argue with the captain anyway. Her crew respected her, protected her and knew that she was as tough as any of the boys and could play in the dirt with the best of them.

The assignment was expected to take a little over a month and the ranger's cabin closest to the area she was needed to oversee was only about forty miles southeast of her Sandpark Point home. She could already feel the forest calling her. She loved the smell of the trees and the clean mountain air. She loved everything about the forest.

With that thought, she rose from the bed, anticipating her much needed escape. She smoothed the much abused pillow.

All she had to do was pack up her gear, load her truck and set out for the wilds of the Cascades. Although she always looked forward to the forest, this particular assignment was one she wished wasn't necessary. It was more disturbing than most. The U.S. Forest Service had a lead on a group of poachers who were responsible for the senseless killing of a number of wild animals in the area. It had been going on for several weeks and as far as anyone had been able to ascertain, the carcasses had been left untouched with no trophies taken. Her assignment was to comb the woods and if she found them, detain the poachers for prosecution.

If there was anything Elaine felt stronger about than her love for the forest, it was her duty to protect it and the wildlife that called it home. She thought for a moment about the poachers and how sorry they would be when she found them. She couldn't prevent the smile that tugged at her lips, but it was short-lived. There was supposed to be a botanist in the area doing research too and she had little doubt that some of her time would be spent babysitting.

Although she wasn't exactly thrilled with the notion of dealing with some whiney lab geek, it was better than being stuck indoors at headquarters. She'd much rather spend her time in her favorite place on earth…the mountains of Washington State.

She packed her neatly ironed olive green uniforms. She would much rather wear jeans than her federal issue uniform pants, but she knew there were bound to be times when they would be necessary so she opted to pack only a few pair of regulation pants and then added some jeans to her bag, making sure to include her favorite, most comfortable pair of Levis. She may be a ranger, but by God she was going to be comfortable.

She grabbed her toiletries and her hairbrush and tossed them into the bag. She made several trips back and forth to the truck as she composed a mental list of things that she still needed to do. Brad was going to pick up her mail and water her plants. She smiled to herself. At least she could always count on her crew. None of the eight men and women under her command had known about Grace's infidelity and Elaine knew that fact had been by design. If they had known, it was a certainty that she would not have been left in the dark. She was as loyal to her crew as they were to her and she loved them all like family. When the office gossip finally reached them, they had all offered their unconditional support. In some ways, this assignment would allow her to escape not only her embarrassment, but the pity she saw in the eyes of her beloved crew.

She double-checked the items she had gathered. She had made sure to pack plenty of cold weather gear. The weather in the mountains in late March could be unpredictable and it wasn't her intention to be unprepared, even if she did have the comforts of a nice cabin at her disposal. Once she was satisfied that she had not forgotten anything else, she locked up her house and climbed in her truck. She would have to make a few stops for supplies and make a few calls, but those could be made from her cell phone on her way out of Sandpark Point. Now that she'd put all thoughts of Grace aside and accepted that the relationship came to an end not only because it was time, but because it was what she had wanted, she was more than ready to get out of town and to the heaven awaiting her.

"Jesus, this is beautiful," Elaine mumbled to herself, several hours later. Spring was a picturesque season at this elevation. Wildflowers were starting to dust the roadsides and the trees were regaining their beautiful hues and bursting with buds just waiting to blossom.

Elaine didn't get out to this part of the Cascades very often, at least not as often as she would have liked, but the beauty of northern Washington wasn't lost on her. The mountains, the trees, the smell of the ocean air in the distance that mingled with the moist forest floor were surreal. This was definitely going to be good for her. She would enjoy the solitude and the opportunity to process the recent events in her life. It would also afford her the opportunity to get away from all the drama and scandal surrounding her breakup with Grace. She couldn't stand drama.

As she drove up the winding access road to the forestry cabin, she looked out over the Tillamook Canyon and was reminded of why she had become a ranger. Not that she ever truly needed to be reminded, but the view was breathtaking. This assignment was a blessing. The best part, no Grace! Hell, no women period.

She spent a good twenty minutes opening up and airing out the ranger's cabin. It hadn't been occupied over the harsh winter and things had become old and stale. The main room was large with an old worn, but reasonably comfortable couch.

There was a huge bed against the opposite wall which was built to accommodate some of the larger burly men she worked with. The mattress probably needed to be aired out but the damn thing would be a pain in the ass to move. She decided to improvise. She might not be a girly-girl, but she certainly knew how to use linen freshener. Fresh sheets and blankets would make it much more inviting when it came time to retire for the night.

She had almost forgotten how nice, almost luxurious, this cabin was compared to most. Some of the cabins were little more than a one-room shed with a small fireplace and bed. Of course, those were intended for shorter assignments or unexpected stays. The rangers who found themselves assigned to this particular cabin referred to it as the Taj Mahal. Each cabin had a government issued structure number, but Elaine and her crew just referred to them by their nicknames.

The wall to her right and perpendicular to the bed had a large stone fireplace and next to that was a door that led into a small bathroom. She was thankful that although there wasn't a bathtub, she would be able to take hot showers. When you worked for the Forest Service for as many years as she had, you didn't take running water for granted.

Just to the left of the cabin door was a small kitchen area

equipped with an electric stove and refrigerator that would work just fine once she got the generator running. Next to the stove was a huge pantry that she knew would still be partially stocked with canned goods. She would have to let the refrigerator cool down for a few hours before transferring the food from the ice chests she had brought. The front wall of the kitchen had large windows that overlooked the canyon below. There was a forestry issue radio that sat on a small table between the main door and the door that led out onto the observation deck. Just glancing out the windows at the view took her breath away. The deck would allow her a perfect vantage point for telltale signs of people in the closer woods—smoke, sudden flights of birds and so on— without having to hike up to the lookout tower.

Best of all, the overlook provided an unobstructed view of the eastern ridge and the basin below. She stepped out onto the deck and took in the Chinook River reflecting the sunlight into the clear blue sky. She took a deep breath and was thankful to have the clean fresh air fill her lungs. There was no cigarette smoke, no perfume, no stares or whispers…nothing to remind her of Grace.

She made multiple trips up and down the wooden steps between the cabin and her truck. She hadn't thought she had brought that much stuff. She planned only to be at the cabin for a little over a month, but after unloading the four ice chests, the canned goods and fresh vegetables she had bought en route, along with her clothing, toiletries, bedding and rifle, she felt as if she were moving in.

Elaine looked around outside before pulling the truck under the deck. The building had been built into the side of the mountain with tall beams that supported the deck and formed a carport. The last ranger had provided a dry stack of wood before departing his post. She noted that she would need to remember to return the favor before she left the cabin. The propane that was remaining combined with the emergency supply she had brought would be more than enough to run the generator until she met up with Donovan to replenish her supplies. Donovan had been part of her crew the longest and he would be her direct correspondent should she need any unexpected supplies. He would also be working the area north of her cabin searching for the poachers by day, while returning home at night. His wife and five kids wanted him home at night and Elaine completely understood and issued him evening or overnight duties only when necessary.

She pulled one of the fuel tanks out of the back of the truck and toted it into the adjacent storage area housing the generator. Once she'd checked the gauges to be sure there had been no tampering and leaks, she started the generator with little effort. She knew she could count on her crew to follow not only her orders, but the directives set by the U.S. Forest Service when it came to maintaining their equipment. All her crew members balked at the task, but it was better than answering to the captain if it wasn't done. Elaine found it amusing that the men on her crew complained more about it than any of the women. But they all knew that in an emergency situation, it was essential that all cabins be ready.

After carrying the rest of the propane tanks into the storage area, she replaced the padlock on the door, gathered an armful of wood and returned to the cabin. There was still a small pile of wood inside and with the armload she had carried in, she was confident she would have plenty to keep the cabin warm all night and well into the next day.

Once settled in, she turned on the radio. She checked in with the ranger station letting them know that she had arrived. She left the radio on and gave it a cursory glance before moving back out onto the deck. Walking to the edge she rubbed her hands along the railing enjoying the rough wood beneath her hands.

After another deep breath, she felt the pressures of her everyday life fade. A narrow trail led down to the river below and about a quarter of a mile from where the trail ended was Big Rock Natural Spring. She thought that if the weather held she would hike down and take a swim tomorrow. She knew that the water would be cold, if not freezing, but it would be refreshing and she looked forward to it. She looked out over the rolling greens darkening as the sun began its descent and accepted the reality of how their relationship had evolved and realized that they were simply not meant to be together.

One of the hardest parts for Elaine would be to forgive herself for not ending the relationship the moment she recognized she wasn't happy and wasn't in love with Grace. She would spend this time of isolation trying to forgive and move on.

The last glimmer of sunlight disappeared, leaving the horizon painted with a thin line of orange. As the full chill of the evening air finally penetrated her clothes, she realized that she had been single for a very long time, but had been unwilling to admit it to herself or anyone else.

Tomorrow she would take her swim in the fresh mountain spring and let nature cleanse her body, mind and soul. Tonight she would be content to sit by a nice warm fire, snuggled in her favorite pajamas with a cup of hot tea.

Devon heated water over her campfire and opened one of the freeze-dried packets she had brought. Reconstituted noodles weren't really food and it didn't sound the least bit appetizing, but tonight it would have to suffice if she wanted the grumbling in her stomach to cease. She had learned to tolerate the tasteless packets out of necessity. They enabled her to pack plenty of meals and she didn't have to worry so much about attracting animals, but the freeze-dried meals always made her look forward to going home and eating real food.

She forced down her so-called dinner and secured its packaging in an airtight bag. Since this was a restricted area, unfortunately there were no bear resistant garbage cans or food storage lockers which forced her to be creative. After checking her campsite one last time to make certain that everything was secure and she hadn't left anything out that might draw curious animals, she crawled into her tent to don the sweats she would sleep in. She really wished that she could shower, but that would have to wait until the next day when the sun could warm her solar shower. She was in no mood for an ice-cold shower tonight. Leaving her moccasins in the vestibule of her tent she secured the door flap before crawling into the warm bedding.

After fulfilling her promise and checking in with Stacey and getting a tinny and crackling but understandable update on Raine's prenatal checkup, Devon snapped her phone closed and with a long yawn snuggled in for the night. She listened to the nightlife of the forest come alive, the sounds of nature calming her with their peaceful rhythm until she was lulled to sleep.

As she stood on the deck and drank a cup of cocoa, Elaine surveyed the area one last time before retiring for the evening. The night was peaceful and the stars bright and so clear that she had opted for a cup of cocoa on the deck rather than tea next to the fire. She couldn't get enough of the cool crisp nights that allowed her to enjoy her flannel pajama pants, huge comfy sweatshirt and fuzzy bear slippers. The cold temperature had forced her to wear her parka which she pulled tighter around her. Only after several years of wear had the government issue parka become a favorite, transforming from stiff and abrasive to being silky-soft and broken in perfectly.

As she let the cold air fill her lungs she could tell there was another storm on its way. She could smell the moisture in the gentle breeze. The moon was bright and reflecting off the top of the pines.

What the hell? She scanned the basin again. The moonlight was sufficiently bright for her to see the plume of smoke wafting up from the trees. It was obviously from a campfire.

"Who would be stupid enough to be up here this time of year and camping, no less?" The botanist hadn't checked in yet so Elaine knew he couldn't be the culprit. Those geeky lab guys weren't exactly known for roughing it.

"Of all the stupid idiotic things to do. I swear if that is those fucking poachers, their asses are mine! Why in the hell would they draw that much attention? Why not just send me a map to their whereabouts?" Nobody answered, of course and Elaine gave herself a self-conscious shake—talking to herself was a habit that came with the job.

They are slaughtering animals on federal land, she reminded herself furiously. As if courting federal charges isn't stupid enough. She took a deep breath trying to calm herself. She would check it out tomorrow when she hiked down to the stream. If it was her poachers, she wanted to be safe and nab them in the light of day. At the very least, whoever it was would definitely receive a citation for an illegal campfire. *That's for damn sure!*

She was almost certain the smoke was coming from the area surrounding the environmental spill site that she and her crew had worked the year before. She knew the area well having spent weeks there in the aftermath of the accident.

If the woods weren't still wet from recent rainfall, she would be more concerned about a fire, but it was highly unlikely that anything would ignite. She decided this was a problem that could be handled in the morning as she pulled her arms tighter across her chest and took another sip of her cocoa.

Chapter 2

Elaine awoke just as the sun crested Somerset Peak behind her to the east. It was late for her to start her day—she would have to set an alarm since the shadow of the mountain made sunrise artificially late and she couldn't always depend on her internal clock to wake her. Filling her cup to the brim with coffee, she stepped out onto the deck. An appreciation for the strength of her coffee was lost on everyone else, but for her it was perfect. It was the only way to jumpstart her day. She looked back in the vicinity of where the smoke had been the night before and the morning sky was clear. Whoever had been there had probably pulled out by now. She took a sip from the steaming mug and sighed appreciatively. She usually had to get her coffee on the run in a travel cup. This morning she mindlessly fingered the ceramic cup with the chipped handle and appreciated the peace.

While Elaine dressed she caught a glimpse of herself in her complete ranger's uniform in the mirror and was reminded of why she had become a ranger. It wasn't necessarily the uniform, although she felt a profound sense of pride when wearing it, especially now that she was captain, but it was more for what her uniform represented. The Cascades were in her blood. They had been here for thousands of years before her and they would continue to be here long after she was gone, but while she was alive, she would help to protect them from people who didn't appreciate their majestic beauty.

Elaine finished her second cup of coffee and set it gently in the sink. She chose to leave her rifle at the cabin and opted for her holster instead, attaching it firmly to her belt. She slung her pack over her shoulder, already filled with a towel, brush and bottled water and headed out the door into the crisp new day.

There wasn't much more than a deer trail leading down into the basin and she was thankful for the thickness of her uniform. The underbrush was still a little thin but it tore at her. This summer, hundreds of thousands of these acres would be a prime feeding ground for wildfire. Elaine knew that she should search for the campsite, but no evidence of fire in the morning made it likely the culprits were gone, so there was little urgency.

The area where she had seen smoke was in the opposite direction of the spring. She had built up a slight perspiration and the fresh cold water was calling for her. She had been anticipating this swim since her arrival the evening before. She wanted to wash away all thoughts of the old and embrace the new.

From the edge of a large boulder above the sparkling natural spring, she shed all of her clothing and plunged into the water. The cold was a welcome shock. After a few minutes her teeth quit chattering and the goose bumps faded from her nude body. She dunked her head in the water and as she came up for air she could feel all the worries and tension that she had been harboring wash away and with it the heaviness that she hadn't even realized had been resting upon her.

She spent several more minutes in the water before pulling herself up onto a rock to let the air dry her. The sun felt good on her naked body although the breeze was cool. In a few months it would be the perfect temperature to skinny dip and then sunbathe. Just the thought made her smile. Sometimes it was the simple pleasures that made life so wonderful.

A quick search of her bag produced her towel and brush. She ran the brush through her hair and looked up at the afternoon sky. As she dressed she could feel the temperature dropping. She would have to get a move on if she was going to locate the illegal campsite from the night before, make sure it was vacated or cite the idiot for the campfire and get back up to the cabin before the cold front arrived.

She felt fresh and new, alive and wonderful for the first time in…well, she couldn't remember how long. She felt like her old self again; the Elaine that had existed before Grace. Feeling completely alone on the mountain and a little bit impish, she chose to leave her undergarments off and enjoyed the soft, worn material of her uniform against her flesh. She was due for new uniforms but there was nothing like a good old-fashioned pair of broken in pants, making it hard for her to part with them. It was like when she slipped on her favorite pair of Levis. They were faded and had holes all over, but as far as she was concerned, they were perfect.

She secured her pack to her shoulders and set out in the general direction that the smoke had come from. As she approached the spill area, she was pleased to see how well the foliage was recovering. The land between the Entiat River and Chiwawa was coming back to life. It had changed, maybe forever, but in her heart she doubted it. In her experience, nature always seemed to find a way to heal itself. A few years before, there had been a similar spill on the upper Sacramento River. Hazmat crews and rangers had worked tirelessly to clean the area. It had taken years to see even a partial recovery and it still had not returned to what it once was. Man's assault on nature, accidental or not, broke Elaine's heart.

As she followed the path, she suddenly heard a voice. She

couldn't ascertain what was being said, the words weren't clear enough, but she followed the sound. She was surprised to realize that it was a woman's voice. She seemed to be having a one-sided conversation, because whoever she was speaking to wasn't answering.

Elaine homed in on the voice. She had every intention of finding out why this woman was out here. *Did she not understand that this was a protected area? Was she illiterate and incapable of reading the warning signs? Did she not get that just by being here she was endangering her own safety?* Whatever the situation, Elaine was going to get rid of her.

She caught sight of a slender figure as she approached, back to her. She glanced around and, not seeing anyone else, assumed the woman was alone. She heard the woman continue talking to herself and watched as she stood for a moment, running her hands though dark hair that just brushed her shoulders.

She must have made a noise because the woman suddenly became aware of her, spinning around on her heels with a startled gasp.

"Hey! What the hell are you doing? Do you know what kind of damage you may be causing? Watch your step!"

Dumbfounded, Elaine quickly glanced down at her feet and saw that she was standing on good old-fashioned soil without so much as a leaf trampled beneath her feet. Once she was certain that she was being berated by a crazy woman, she looked up again. This time her breath caught.

Surely this had to be some kind of apparition or maybe a hallucination. This woman was far too beautiful to be real. She blinked, looked again and couldn't stop her gaze as it slowly traveled up her long legs, past her flat stomach and then higher where it rested on her breasts. Even through her fleece and blue jeans, Elaine could tell that she was firm in all the right places and all of her curves were in perfect proportion to her body.

When Elaine finally met the woman's stormy gray eyes, she felt like a small child being chastised for having misbehaved. She was chagrined for having so thoroughly ogled the woman instead of getting right to business and maintaining her professionalism. Did this woman not see her uniform and realize that she had every right to be in these woods? Elaine tried to pull her gaze away, but in spite of her greatest efforts, she felt paralyzed.

Devon held out her hand and snapped, "My name is Devon McKinney and you are?" The husky voice that answered, however, rolled over her senses, disconcerting her.

"Captain Elaine Thomas."

The woman exuded quiet confidence. It was obvious that she was comfortable with her surroundings and her authority and Devon was impressed at the captain insignia on the worn uniform. It was obvious that this woman had been doing her job for a while.

Unbidden, she also realized the uniform was worn in all the right places. The open collar of the ranger's shirt framed a long throat tanned to a delicate gold. It would have been rude to openly stare at the ranger's breasts, but she found it impossible to ignore the taut nipples pressing firmly against the fabric. Her legs, even encased in pants, were clearly tight and muscular. Devon's mouth went suddenly dry when she glanced up only to be met by the darkest eyes and fullest lips she had ever seen. Her pulse quickened as she took in the powerfully attractive woman standing before her with hands on hips.

Noticing her slightly damp auburn hair, she wondered if the ranger had been swimming. In these water temperatures? That was slightly nutty, in her opinion, though there was something to be said about a refreshing dip in frigid waters.

She saw Elaine take notice of the open notebook with her sketches, then her eyes traveled to the tape measure, boring rod and knapsack full of instruments.

"What are you researching?"

Devon withheld her mild amusement of the very perceptive observation. "I'm examining the growth in the area. There is still poisoned plant life from the toxic spill, but the levels do show a marked decrease." She stopped herself before saying more. It had been her experience that not many people were interested in hearing about her work.

"So you're the botanist?"

She searched Elaine's eyes for mockery or skepticism. They seemed to convey respect for her and her work. She was shocked because it wasn't something that she was accustomed to seeing, except in Stacey or Raine. Most people could care less about botany, but she got the impression that this woman was different. Obviously, being a ranger, her job was to take care of these mountains, but that didn't automatically mean that she gave a damn about the details.

"That's right. I was informed that you were expecting me."

"Yes, but you didn't check in with the ranger's station so I wasn't sure of your arrival time or camp location."

She gave herself a mental slap. Yes, she had forgotten that bit of professional courtesy.

Elaine looked up at the sky between the trees. "There's a storm rolling in. It doesn't feel like snow, but you should probably be careful."

She wanted to bristle, but she squelched the feeling. She reminded herself that this woman was simply doing her job. She didn't know that Devon could take care of herself. She had no idea that Devon had been out in the field more times than she could count.

"There are reports of poachers in the area, so I'll be back to check on you. If you need anything," she turned and pointed, "I'm just up the hill at the cabin."

"Thank you, Captain."

She watched Elaine walk away, hoping she wouldn't turn around and catch her staring. In the slant of the late afternoon sun, Elaine's hair was bronze as it swayed. She gazed at the spot where the woman faded from sight, then with a shiver, finally noticed the dropping temperature. She wasn't sure if the rapid cooling of her body was because the ranger had left or if it was actually the weather. Captain Thomas was right. There was a storm rolling in and judging by the moist air it was most likely going to bring rain.

She gathered up her equipment and headed back to her camp. Now distracted and tired, she decided it was time to call it a day. Who would have thought that she would ever meet anyone up here at this time of year, much less someone so attractive?

She made it back to camp and started a hearty fire just as it began to sprinkle. She sat just inside her tent letting her thoughts wander as she watched the rain dance about the flames. She instinctively knew that Elaine was a lesbian. Somehow that thought was as unsettling as the penetrating gaze and dark eyes that seemed to stare right into her, almost through her.

She sighed to herself. She had work to do and wondering about the attractive ranger wasn't going to help her get it done. As the last of the light faded over the top of the mountains, she secured her camp before returning to her tent where she switched on the lantern and found her notebook.

The notebook drew her eyes to her hands and she shook her head at the dry skin. Her hands were already red and beginning to chap. It was just one of the many hazards of working in the field, but she was never unprepared. She enjoyed the feel of the lotion as it soaked in, rehydrating her skin. She reached into her pack and produced a pencil and began deciphering her notes until the sound of raindrops gently trickling down upon the fabric of the tent soothed her to sleep.

Elaine stoked the fire and went back to the window with her cup of tea. The lightning that danced across the sky was breathtaking. She knew there was a chance of a lightning strike, but the rain cascading down eased her mind. The danger of fire was always at the forefront of any ranger's mind, but in circumstances like this, Elaine didn't have to worry too much. The rain quieted her fears. There was nothing like a high mountain storm and she was reminded of how much she missed just sitting and watching one. She hadn't seen any signs of the poachers or any more of their victims, but decided she should check in with the station anyway.

"Dane, you got a copy?"

"Go ahead, Captain."

"I made contact with the botanist, Devon McKinney. Did she check in with you?"

"Hang on. I'll check the log." Elaine waited patiently for a moment, "No, she didn't."

"So we don't know anything about her?" Just talking about Devon conjured her image and sent a shiver down Elaine's spine.

"Gimme one minute and let me see what I can find out."

Elaine tried to squelch the prickle on the back of her neck as she waited. She told herself that she was just being efficient and knowledge was power. Not to mention, an invaluable tool.

"Well, Captain, it says in our registry that she is a doctor with the EPA and worked the original spill."

No way!

"Was she on one of the follow-up teams?"

There was a moment of silence before Dane finally responded. The tone of his voice had changed slightly. "No, she was one of the first responders."

Okay. Now Elaine was impressed.

"All right, thanks for the information. Please log Dr. McKinney in. She has set up camp at the spill site."

"Will do."

"Thanks, Dane."

She searched her memory as she returned the handset to its former position. There wasn't a single doubt in her mind that had she met Devon before, she would have remembered. Devon was one of the first to respond? Damn, she certainly hadn't expected that.

Elaine retired to the sofa and ate the can of chunky chicken soup that she had prepared for dinner as she tried to push thoughts of Devon from her mind. The next morning she was planning to drive along the old logging road leading to White River. There would be quite a bit of animal movement over there this time of year and it would be an ideal location to search for the poachers.

Elaine shivered as she thought about the senseless slaughter of animals. Most of the animals that were killed in these woods were killed by hunters for their meat. But the most recent rash of killings seemed to be thrill kills. Elaine had no idea how shooting these innocent animals gave anyone a thrill. The poachers she was searching for seemed to be shooting anything they came across. They had found a hawk and other birds, deer, beavers and even squirrels. Some poachers went after bears, but those generally made the news. The majority of animals that were killed went unnoticed, except by the individuals who made a career of protecting them.

She headed for the shower, grateful for the running water and even more grateful that it would be hot. She quickly washed her hair and stood motionless enjoying the water cascading over her body. Knowing that the water would soon turn cold, she finished washing and exited the stall. At least she had a few minutes to enjoy it. The heat from the fire was penetrating the bathroom but it was still chilly. Goose bumps crawled across her skin and she hurriedly slipped into sweats and a long-sleeved shirt. She towel-dried her hair and made a mental note to wash her towel and her uniform the next day. She still had two more clean uniforms, but always wanted to be sure she wouldn't be caught without one. Her clothes rack in front of the fire would allow her laundry to dry faster. She missed some of the comforts of home, but hand washing her clothes beat the hell out wearing them again without a good cleansing.

Curled up on the couch in front of the fire, she brushed out her hair, sifting through it with her fingers hoping it would dry out a little more before bed. She stared into the flames and had a flash of the stormy gray eyes she had stared into earlier in the day. The heat of the fire suddenly seemed cool in contrast to the heat of her body.

She continued to brush her hair and wondered how Devon's hair would feel in her hands. *What the hell am I doing?* She was here for solitude, alone time to enjoy her surroundings and forget about women for God's sake. Thinking about a woman she had just met was the very last thing she should be doing. She finished brushing out the long locks and finally stripped for bed. She tossed her clothes over the back of the couch and slid between the cool sheets, trying not to think about the beautiful botanist.

She finally fell asleep and was thankful that she didn't remember her dreams. She had a feeling they would have featured a certain somebody, making it even harder not to focus on her undeniable attraction.

Chapter 3

Devon chewed thoughtfully on a mint leaf from her pocket as she crouched down to take a soil sample near the base of the *viola glabellas*. She was pleased to see that the smooth, yellow violet would return this year. The young flower seemed to be strong and healthy. Near it, still under the surface, were the beginnings of a *viola sheltonii*. She was surprised to find the Shelton's Violet. They were rare in the northern mountains and the spill had destroyed many of the fairer species. Other, heartier plants, such as the *thalictrum fendleri*, had come back rather quickly and various types of meadow rue were more inclined to survive.

She continued gathering specimens, examining the bark, cork and periderm. She wished that she had indulged in another cup of coffee. She wasn't the biggest fan of instant coffee, but this morning it had tasted unusually good. Maybe it was the way it had warmed her from the inside out. She made a mental note to buy a coffee press so she could brew *real* coffee next time she ventured into the field. Unfortunately, the day moved into midmorning without any rise in temperature and she still had a lot of work to do. She knew she would have to remain focused and pick up her pace.

One of her final tasks on this assignment would be to gather samples to take back to the lab. She would seek out a variety of plants in order to closely examine the vascular cambium through the pith to see how the vegetation was truly responding to the contamination. The foliage that had returned to the area had still been compromised and would need to be studied closely.

She wasn't feeling confident about the trees along the river bank, though, not after boring into several to examine the core. She had not only been studying their age, but the discoloration of the wood. The outer rings had an unnatural rust color. Her cursory inspection of the root system showed damage to the mycorrhiza and she didn't really see any way that the trees would recover, but she had been surprised before. The resilience of nature continually amazed her.

When she got back to the lab and tested the core samples and analyzed the results, she'd have a better indication of the magnitude of the damage. She was hopeful that the poisons would filter out of the soil and with transplanted seedlings the river bank would return to its once lush existence. If the transplant was unsuccessful the future of this area was anyone's guess.

The fertility of the soil was another concern altogether. The hazardous chemicals had leached well into the subsoil. On first inspection, the soil texture hadn't seemed to change all that much, but the death of the flora in the area told a different story. The soil that enabled the vegetation to absorb water, nutrients and oxygen through its roots was now carrying harmful chemicals. The earth had endured a violent biological attack that would have gone largely unnoticed had it not been for the danger to the human population. The South Croix River was a minor tributary to the Columbia River. Had the spill not been contained before reaching the Columbia River, the effects would have been disastrous. As seriously as she took the poisoning of the plant life, just thinking about the possibility that those toxins could have reached people was unimaginable. The damage wouldn't have come close to the scale of the Gulf oil spill, but would have been devastating nonetheless.

The toxins would be filtered and dissipate over time, but their presence would be enough to affect growth for years to come. As she looked around, she was once again sickened by the attacks of terrorism waged on the environment by man. Train tracks had no business running this close to precious woodlands.

She continued to take notes when a noise startled her and she abruptly stopped to listen. For a wild, fleeting moment she hoped that it was the ranger. When she turned around she let out her breath. The only creatures to join her today would be the chipmunks playing tag on the tree branches behind her. Normally she would have been more attuned to the noises surrounding her and not nearly so jumpy. She tried to convince herself that the only reason she wasn't paying more attention was because she was focused on work. The ranger had certainly gotten her attention.

She spent several minutes watching the chipmunks in amusement. They didn't seem to have a care in the world. It had been a long time since she had felt that way. Her social life consisted of spending time with Stacey and her sister, but when she wasn't with them, she was working. Since college, she had been so focused on her career it left her very little time to meet anyone. Sometimes the loneliness made her wonder if the sacrifices she had made to advance her career were really worth it. The truth was she had spent far more time working than was actually necessary. She longed to find the love everyone around her insisted she deserved and would someday find. It was ironic really. She had been on the receiving end of plenty of pickup lines from men. But for reasons she would probably never understand women didn't generally pay her the same attention, at least not the women she would have preferred. That is until she met

Captain Elaine Thomas who had looked at her in a way she had always imagined. It was almost inconceivable that a woman of Elaine's caliber had looked at her that way.

She had spent years learning to work with the U.S. Forest Service and the National Park Service. She respected both agencies and knew in her heart that they did the best they could to protect these areas. But as she took in the beauty around her she was sickened by the people responsible for defiling such a magnificent place. She supposed if it wasn't for people like her and those she worked alongside, all of the forests would be replaced with concrete jungles. People just really had no idea what they were destroying. She knew that she was being judgmental, which wasn't one of her better qualities, but when she looked around all she saw were reminders that civilization wasn't really civil at all.

Devon's Internet service was slow at best, but she knew she was lucky not to have to hike up the mountain to find a signal. She sent a short e-mail to Stacey just as she had promised and was happy to receive one from Raine letting her know that all the news from the obstetrician was okay. The same message was reiterated by Stacey who had left her an e-mail detailing her daily checks on Raine.

Stacey went on to tell her that her houseplants were coming along nicely. She had planted a new fern and Devon shouldn't worry, Stacey would take care of it. She laughed to herself. If it wasn't for Stacey, she would have a gravel yard and fake plants. She felt it embarrassing that she couldn't seem to keep a houseplant off death row and she was a botanist for the love of God!

She returned a few other e-mails and loaded some pictures onto her laptop. As soon as she finished, she turned off the computer so to not run down the battery. She lay back on her bed and finally admitted that she had been hoping to see the ranger again today. Of course she hadn't. She knew that Elaine had work to do and that she probably wouldn't be back anytime soon.

Besides, she told herself, there was no reason for her to want to see the ranger. She didn't want company. She enjoyed these quiet days working. That's why she preferred to work alone. She could have worked with a team if she wanted, but she enjoyed the solitude. No, there was no reason that she should want to see Elaine again.

Elaine spent the next several days driving the fire lanes to check out areas where there was an abundance of animal activity that a poacher might decide was prime killing ground. So far she had seen no evidence of the poachers, but she knew that could change at any time.

In another month or two logging would begin on the west side of the basin and following the loggers would be a crew planting seedlings. She knew that it was just a fact of life that as long as there were trees, people would cut them down. At least there would be foresters coming in to replant. Hopefully the presence of so many people would help keep illegal activities to a minimum.

For the most part, the old growth regions would go untouched. The areas that were stripped with heavy equipment were less beautiful, but they did succeed in removing the heavy foliage that could cause a fire to burn out of control or suffocate any new growth. People like her made sure that corporate forestry stayed in its allowed areas, though sometimes it was an ugly business.

The North Cascades National Park began just to the north of the Wenatchee National Forest...Elaine's territory. The U.S. Forest Service was a branch of the Department of Agriculture and was charged with protecting National Forests and grasslands. Elaine and the other rangers focused mainly on controlling forest fires, conservation and protecting the quality of the environment so that future generations could enjoy it. The Forest Service had to work in concert with the National Park Service; a sector of the Department of the Interior. They were responsible not only for National Parks, but also recreational areas and historical sites. They may have shared the same mission, protecting the land, but didn't always see eye to eye. Generally, the Park Service had more contact with the public and as Elaine had been reminded many times, the millions of visitors to National Parks each year made a significant contribution to the economy. She didn't envy the park rangers who had to deal so frequently with tourists. That's one reason why she had decided on the U.S. Forest Service. It wasn't that she didn't believe that protecting people was as important as protecting the land, it was that deep inside the forest she felt comfortable. Specializing in law enforcement and firefighting kept her out of most of the politics too. It was home.

Elaine glanced at her watch. It had been several days and she knew she should check in on Dr. McKinney. Tomorrow she would need to do that. She tried, in vain, to convince herself that she was just doing her job, but the quickening of her heartbeat when she reflected on their first brief encounter was both terrifying and exhilarating. As she surveyed the area, she noticed the flush of her cheeks in the rearview mirror and rolled down her window to let in a cold breeze.

Elaine rose early, dressed and was ready to head out with the rising of the sun. She hadn't slept very well and had awoken several times throughout the night. It was going to be a beautiful day and she was just anxious to face it. Yes, surely that was it. It certainly didn't have anything to do with Devon McKinney.

Elaine was well down the trail when she paused. She had always tried to be honest with herself, although she hadn't always been successful. But still she didn't consciously lie to herself and she wasn't going to start now. She knew her inner voice was right.

She shifted the rifle on her shoulder to stop it from bumping her canteen. She was acting like a greenhorn, fumbling nervously. There was nothing wrong with being curious about someone. Why wouldn't she be curious about the most attractive woman she had ever met? She wiped her suddenly sweaty palms on her pants before continuing on.

Elaine arrived at Devon's camp just as Devon was slinging a pack onto her shoulder. "Going somewhere?"

Devon spun around on her heel, looking both startled and shocked, but the slow smile that spread across Devon's face made Elaine's stomach suddenly jump and she immediately became aware of the slight perspiration between her breasts.

"Just going down the river a bit to gather some data."

Elaine repositioned the rifle on her shoulder. "I'll walk with you."

Devon's mouth opened and closed as though she was going to protest, but instead she simply nodded and mumbled, "All right."

They walked in silence for several minutes. Elaine was taking note of the way Devon unconsciously avoided stepping on plants, much the way she herself did. She was delighted that she didn't have to slow her pace for Devon who kept up easily.

"How's the research coming?"

Devon dodged a tree. "Some of the foliage away from the river's edge is promising, but I won't really know until I can get some samples back to the lab."

"When do you head back?"

"I need to have everything finished up here in about three to four weeks."

"Do you think that's enough time? The last researcher was up here for almost two months."

"It has to be." At Elaine's inquisitive stare, Devon went on to explain.

"My sister is pregnant and she's due in about six weeks, but the doctor thinks she might deliver early. There's no way I'm going to miss that."

Elaine digested the information. "Congratulations. First time aunt?"

"Yes. I'm so excited. I would have delayed this assignment, but my sister insisted that I come. I've learned not to argue with her, especially now that she's eight months pregnant."

"I'm a little surprised that you are on this assignment solo. I didn't think the EPA would let you come up here alone, especially at this time of year."

Devon arched an eyebrow as her mouth spread into a slow grin. Sarcasm tainted her voice as she replied, "Yeah well, I'm rogue."

Elaine shook with laughter. The sound filled the trees and reverberated around them. "A rogue botanist!"

Devon gave a toss of the head, a crooked smile showing her amusement and kept walking.

It was some time before she stopped to settle her pack on a large rock. "This is where I need to start. Thank you for the company."

Devon stood just a step from Elaine. Elaine knew her own lips were slightly parted. The hike was not why her breath was shallow and her eyes unfocused. If she didn't get it together, Devon would think she was a freak. She couldn't stop looking at Devon's lips.

Devon did seem to be breathing hard from the hike. Her chest rose and fell rapidly as she stared back at Elaine. So Elaine did the only thing that made sense. She said, "Have a good day," before turning and walking off.

Devon worked until the sun set each night for the next several days. Hours of squatting had caused knots in her thighs, but the ground was far too cold to sit on. She could feel the moisture gathering in the air. It wasn't heavy enough for rain or snow yet, but she knew that it was coming. She wanted to get as much work done before the weather changed and it helped that she saw no more of the captain.

She made sure to call Stacey and Raine on the designated nights. The static from the absence of cell towers and rough terrain made it difficult to maintain a signal, forcing her to keep the calls short and left her wondering how her sister was really doing. If she felt disconnected from Raine, she could only imagine how her husband Phillip felt, getting all his news while stationed in Iraq. She knew the days were getting longer, but the added minute each morning and each night weren't doing much to help her meet her deadline.

Her work was moving along at a snail's pace thanks to the hard earth. It was still frozen and difficult to penetrate. Of course, she had expected it, but it made doing research tedious. Still she was able to examine root structures and color. A light mist was forming on the foliage when she finally decided to spend some time in her tent transferring her data to her computer. Her backpacker's solar-based charging unit would give her well over two hours of battery life.

The graphs and charts that she had made to compare to last year's samples showed improvement, but the further she worked downriver the worse her findings. The hazmat team had arrived by helicopter within minutes of the reported derailment and worked as quickly as possible to erect a barrier. The one break they did catch was that it was a slow water season and the water level was low compared to other times during the year. In an attempt to prevent the chemical from reaching the Columbia River, they had placed absorption socks along the surface of the water. Luckily they had been successful in restricting the contamination to the South Croix River, but the result was that it had provided a smaller area for the pollutant to collect, causing more intense damage to this area of the river. The accumulation of the toxins had taken a serious toll on the plant life and Devon was disheartened by the data she collected.

Chapter 4

Elaine spent the next four days staying busy and searching for the poachers. But no matter how busy she remained, Devon McKinney invaded her thoughts. How could she even think about Devon when she had decided that a break from women was exactly what she needed, especially after the way things ended with Grace? She had planned on taking some time to be single and free of the complications that women bring. But what she hadn't planned on was Devon.

Her mind replayed the events of the last time she had seen Devon, standing on the river bank gazing into Devon's eyes, focusing on those perfectly luscious lips that made her heart race. When she looked at Devon she felt an unfamiliar heat radiate through her body.

Like the previous days, she decided to circumvent Devon's camp. In order to avoid Devon's campsite, she was forced to take a much harder trail along the ridge, but it was worth it. Devon was not going to disrupt her thoughts further.

She had decided when she awoke that morning that another dip in the cold mountain spring was definitely in order. God knew that she needed something to cool her imagination and her body. Her dreams had been far too graphic for her liking. Once she regained control of her libido then maybe she would be able to act like the professional she was.

Elaine made her way down the mountainside toward the deep clear pool. Her forearms glistened with sweat and she looked forward to the cold water. She followed the water's edge down to a large boulder that stood between her and the pool. She had barely reached the top when she froze.

Elaine's mouth went completely dry as she took in the sight before her. Light shimmered off the water, hiding and then revealing the near perfect body just beneath the surface. Devon was on the far end lying in the shallows of the crystal clear water.

Devon heard the motion on the rock and lay still for several minutes listening for another sound. She finally rolled over and slowly swam toward the bank. The last thing she wanted to do was share the water with an animal. As she lifted herself from the water and began to move toward her clothes she caught a reflection in the water. The image was unmistakable. Elaine stood above, only partially hidden by a tree, in her faded green uniform, sun glistening off her ginger-colored hair.

Devon smiled to herself. If the ranger thought she was going to chase her off then she was sorely mistaken. When she had first met the ranger and noticed her dampened hair, she had been reminded of the crystal clear spring. Although it was bitterly cold, it was invigorating. Devon didn't consider her lack of clothing as she dove back into the water. As she surfaced, she threw her head back letting her hair cascade down over her shoulders. She stood with the water just under her breasts. Almost immediately, her body had been anesthetized by the cold water and she hadn't noticed just how erect her nipples were. She glanced down, looking for Elaine's reflection, when she noticed the state of her breasts. She mentally shrugged. Oh well, there wasn't much she could do about it now. She had to admit she was flattered. She imagined most women might have been annoyed or even furious under the same circumstances, but she was oddly appreciative that Elaine continued to watch.

She knew that Elaine was still on the rock as she continued her swim and that Elaine didn't realize that she had been spotted. If Elaine wanted the pool then she could damn well wait her turn, or at the very least announce herself. She was enjoying taking a break from her work and she wasn't going to be chased away just because Elaine wanted to swim and couldn't share.

Devon made several more laps around the pool. Using her muscles this way was a welcome change to the positions she held while working. Occasionally Devon would roll over to float on her back enjoying the sun. She knew that she should probably be polite and let Elaine have the pool soon, but she was here first damn it and she was going to enjoy her time. She reminded herself that was her only motivation for staying in the freezing water.

Elaine was careful not to make another sound. She knew that she should leave. It wasn't right watching Devon this way. If their positions had been reversed, she would be irritated that she was being watched. Wouldn't she? But her eyes were fixed and she was powerless over them.

Devon's body was even more beautiful than she had imagined. She was surprised to see just how tan Devon was…everywhere. She was willing to bet that smooth bronze wasn't from a tanning bed.

As Devon swam around the pool, she couldn't help but

35

memorize her graceful movements. The fluid motion created a throbbing between her legs as she imagined how that body would feel moving against her own.

When Devon surfaced from the water Elaine felt like she was in a slow-motion movie. She watched as the water dripped from Devon's face and ran down her neck. She was envious of the beads of water that caressed Devon's breasts as they made their way back to the pool. Elaine couldn't help but follow the path of the water with her eyes. One drop clung to Devon's nipple and she wanted nothing more than to take it in her mouth.

She barely stifled a gasp when Devon finally made her way out of the water. She reached down to pick up a towel when Elaine finally noticed the tattoo on her left shoulder. It was the only mark on her otherwise perfect body. Elaine couldn't see it clearly, but it definitely made her want to see it close up and in detail. Too soon it was hidden below clothing, but that didn't stop Elaine from recalling it perfectly.

The last thing she expected was a sudden devilish smile flashed her way, with a cheeky, "It's all yours, Captain."

For several minutes Elaine stood stupefied, feeling like a Peeping Tom who had just been caught by the object of her desire. She didn't know how she would ever be able to look Devon in the face again.

Chapter 5

Elaine continued her meticulous scouring north along the ridge, looking for any signs of poachers while she studiously ignored the existence of Devon McKinney. She spent a couple of days in the observation tower scanning for plumes of smoke, anything that would indicate campers, other than Devon, in the forest. She was due to connect with Donovan at the end of this sweep. She was doing her job, no distractions.

Right.

She resigned herself to the fact that her conscience wasn't going to leave her alone. She would have to head down the mountain and apologize to Devon for watching her. She shivered at the thought of seeing Devon again.

She had tried to push thoughts of Devon from her mind, but the images of her wet body haunted her. She had memorized every inch and now she was paying the price with utter distraction. She finally gave in and let her mind wander free to fantasize about the sexy doctor.

There had been many women she had found attractive, but Devon was exquisite. Never before had she been so drawn to another woman and never had she been forced relentlessly to fight the desire to keep her distance.

It wasn't just Devon's body that attracted her. There was something in her eyes. How could a woman she didn't even know seem to be staring directly into her? When Devon looked at her, Elaine felt truly *seen*.

She met Donovan on schedule at the bottom of the service road for supplies and asked for any word that the poachers might have moved on.

"Sorry, Captain, but a couple of hikers found a deer lying in the middle of a field about a half a mile north of here. I checked it out, but I lost the trail."

"Thanks, Donovan. Keep me posted if you find anything."

Donovan gave her one of his endearing smiles. She cared for all the members of her crew, but Brad and Donovan held a special place in her heart. They had worked together for years, even before she had made captain and they had been in some pretty hairy situations together. Besides knowing that both of them had her back, regardless of the situation, neither of them tried to bullshit her and they both treated her with the utmost respect.

When she had finally made captain, they were the first to congratulate her. She had been with the service longer than either of the men and she knew their words were sincere.

Donovan looked up at the sky. "I brought you extra supplies. I figure you will be snowed in before too long if the latest weather report is accurate."

She smiled at him. He was always looking out for her. She was the boss and he acted like he was her older brother. "Thanks, Donovan. I really appreciate it."

She was almost back to her truck when his voice stopped her. "Hey, Cap?"

"Yeah?"

"Be careful up there."

She gave him a reassuring smile. "Don't worry, I will. You do the same."

She slowly drove back up to the cabin. She would need to check the fuel level in the generator and restock her supply of wood. The food that Donovan had given her would last her for quite awhile. She glanced at what he had brought and smiled. Along with the canned goods, he had made sure to bring plenty of meat. The box included the customary ground beef and deli-sliced lunchmeat, but also included two choice New York Strip steaks and a few pork chops. She was particularly surprised to find that he had even remembered to include applesauce, which she loved to eat with her pork chops. She wasn't much of a breakfast person, although she loved her morning coffee and he often preached to her about the importance of eating breakfast. She wasn't terribly surprised to find that he had made a point of adding turkey sausage, eggs, instant oatmeal and bagels to her order of coffee. *Real subtle, Donovan.* He had even added fresh fruits and vegetables. Leave it to Donovan; she would certainly be eating well! Too bad her meals would be unaccompanied.... Oh, hell, she was thinking about Devon again.

She stopped the truck and closed her eyes, taking a deep breath. She couldn't remember ever being attracted to Grace or any other woman, the way she was attracted to Devon. Her hands shook slightly as she held the steering wheel. Even now her body warmed as she thought about Devon. Her body's response frightened her.

She allowed herself a smile, though, as she thought about Devon's parting words. Devon had known that she was there the whole time and hadn't let on. She had been stunned by the flirtatious smile that Devon had thrown over her shoulder. *Damn, that woman has a wicked sense of humor, but I still have to apologize for the Peeping Tom act I pulled.*

She reached Devon's camp early the next morning. Everything was quiet and she wasn't sure if Devon had left already or if she was still asleep. She was flustered by the situation, wanting to apologize and leave as quickly as possible. She was humiliated enough as it was, she didn't want to have to seek out the other woman in order to accomplish her mission. She couldn't just stand here and imagine Devon asleep on the other side of the tent wall, hair mussed, face relaxed.

She had decided the only thing she could do was leave, but had gone only a few feet when she spied Devon kneeling on a large rock just up the river. She couldn't quite make out what the woman was doing, but it certainly looked as though Devon was about to go headfirst into the water. Elaine didn't think as she instinctively ran toward her.

Devon was reaching for her clipboard as Elaine clamped down on her leg. She swiveled her body around and nearly shouted, "What in the hell are you doing?"

Elaine shook her head. Great, now the woman probably thought that not only was she a peeping pervert, but that she was inclined to accost women as well! She quickly released her leg. "You looked like you were about to fall in."

"I'm perfectly fine, thank you very much!"

Devon's angry frown suddenly changed into wide-eyed panic. She wobbled, flailed for Elaine, clipboard clattering down between the rocks.

Elaine grabbed her leg and again shifted her weight back to stop Devon's forward descent.

"Twist around here and give me your hand."

Devon did as she was told. Her shirt had slipped up and a fair amount of her stomach was exposed.

Elaine had a flash of her in the pool and damn near dropped her.

Devon looked alarmed again. "Are you sure we aren't both going to go tumbling in?"

"Do you doubt me?"

Devon looked back at the water and then back at Elaine, who was now kneeling between Devon's legs. Her disorientation faded into a teasing smile. "Seems like I'm in no position to doubt you."

Elaine grinned as she took Devon's hand. In one swift motion she pulled Devon up while standing to free her legs. Devon recovered her clipboard and they both climbed off the rock.

Once on terra firma, Devon said, "It would seem that I owe you a thank you."

Elaine managed to say casually, "Just doing my job."

Devon laughed. "Your job is to scare women off rocks so that you can rescue them?"

"Only on good days." Elaine hoped she sounded wicked or enticing or anything but stupid. She couldn't help the flirtatious little wink that she added. She felt her stomach tighten at Devon's sharp intake of breath.

Devon half turned away to stare at the trail. "What brings you to my home away from home?"

Elaine's bravado faded. "I owe you an apology…for…uh… for the other day."

Devon shrugged. "Accepted."

Elaine's eyes widened. "That's it?"

"What were you expecting?"

"I don't know. I expected you would be mad." Elaine paused, not knowing what else to say. She certainly didn't want to encourage Devon to be angry. "I guess I should get going."

Without another word, Elaine walked briskly away along the trail into the forest. She could feel Devon's gaze on her back, but it was not the response she had wanted. She wasn't entirely sure what she wanted. But the end result left her feeling like an idiot.

"Hey!" Devon waited for the man to look up at her. They were across the river and he had been leaning down to fill his canteen from the river directly across from her. It took just a

41

moment for Devon to realize there was someone else with him, an attractive woman who also appeared to be in her mid-twenties.

The man finally looked up. "Yeah?"

"You can't drink from there. It's contaminated."

He shrugged at her like she didn't know what she was talking about. She had half a mind to let the fool drink the damn water. Just because he was too stupid to know that, although the surface was running cleaner, the pool he had chosen to fill from was still mostly standing water and would have poisons leaching out of the soil. But she just really couldn't have that on her conscience. If the idiot was going to ignore her she was going to have to get his attention.

She knew that she was in no danger of actually hitting him. So she heaved a large rock in his direction and was lucky that it got close enough to get his attention.

"Damn it, lady. What the hell? We're just going to get a drink and be on our way. What's it to you?"

Where the hell is a good forest ranger when you need one? "Go upriver about a hundred yards and cross over and I'll explain."

Devon could tell that they had heard her because the woman with him prodded him to do as he was told. Though they spoke in low tones, she was pretty sure he had just called her a bitch. She paralleled them on her side of the river until they came to a tree that was half fallen across the river that would lead to some boulders and her side of the river bank.

The woman was far more agile and looking at the two it was clear which one was more outdoorsy. Her boots were well worn in comparison to his, which appeared to be brand new. Her gear seemed to be broken in. If she had to guess, he was out here because he didn't think "the little woman" could do it without him.

Devon waited patiently for them to cross. When they finally made it onto her bank she held out her hand. "Hi. I'm Dr. McKinney."

Devon didn't normally use her title to introduce herself but she wanted to make it clear from the onset of this conversation that she knew what she was talking about. She looked closely at the young man she supposed some women might find attractive, but the man's attitude and scarcely concealed resentment made it difficult for her to see how any woman could tolerate him. The man looked at her with blatant hostility and it was obvious he didn't like taking instruction from women.

The young woman stepped around him, obviously trying to cut him off and keep his rudeness from escalating. "I'm Angela and this is my boyfriend Steve."

Devon shook both of their hands. "I'm sorry for throwing that rock back there but I really needed you *not* to fill your canteen from this part of the river."

Steve's insolence was obvious from his stance, but thankfully it was Angela who held the conversation. "If you don't mind me asking, why is that?"

"This is the spill site from about a year ago. The surface water is starting to run cleaner but there are still toxins in the soil and they leach into the water. You could have gotten very sick even if you did use purification tabs."

Angela gave Steve a look that Devon easily understood. It was clear that Angela thought Steve was an idiot. "Are we really at the spill sight? We are supposed to be about two miles from here."

Devon smiled. "Yes, you really are. But there is a ranger stationed up the mountain there who can probably get you back on track."

Angela looked up the hill as though she was trying to gauge where they would need to go.

Steve took hold of her hand. *Like a dog marking his territory. Men are so damn predictable.* "I'll get us there, honey."

"Like you got us here?" Angela's tone suggested that she'd lost some earlier dispute about their direction.

Oh good God! I so do not need this. Devon looked at her watch. If these two could keep up, she could lead them to Elaine's cabin and she would only lose a day of work. *And I get to see Elaine.* Damn, she really needed to put an end to these thoughts.

Devon smiled as politely as she could knowing that she would probably have to listen to these two bicker all the way up to the cabin. Oh well, once she turned them over to Elaine they wouldn't be her problem. That thought produced a smile.

"Come on."

Angela and Steve continued to argue somewhat quietly behind her as Devon led them back down the river bank. She decided not to waste time by gathering up her tools and putting them away. The sooner she was rid of these two the better. Instead, she grabbed her daypack and slung it over her shoulder and indicated they should follow her.

Halfway up the mountain the bickering ended and Devon suspected that had a lot to do with the fact that Steve was winded. She thought about taking a break for his sake, but Angela seemed to have no problem keeping up and they really needed to keep moving if she was going to get back to her campsite before the sun set.

Not to mention, it didn't seem like a good idea to put herself unnecessarily in Elaine's company when she had a deadline. Her schedule was tight and babies didn't wait on anything. When they are ready, they come at a moment's notice.

"So Dr. McKinney, what are you doing up here?"

Devon turned and flashed a quick smile at the young woman. She wondered when curiosity would set in. "I'm a botanist with the EPA and I'm collecting samples to study how much regeneration has taken place and how badly the plant life has been affected."

"So you're studying the water as well as the foliage along the river?"

"That's right."

"Hey, wait. You're Dr. *Devon* McKinney?"

Devon stopped and turned around. Steve immediately leaned against a tree breathing hard and obviously thankful for the break no matter how brief it might be. "That's right. How did you know?"

Angela flashed a smile as though she had just unlocked one of life's great mysteries. "You were quoted in one of my biology textbooks last term. I also went to one of your guest lectures at the university. The one Dr. Langford hosted."

Devon thought for a moment. Yes, she remembered that lecture. She hadn't really wanted to present, but her bosses pressured her into it. If there was one thing Devon loathed it was public speaking, but the lecture had seemed to go well enough. Well, obviously it had if this young woman could remember who she was. Devon couldn't list half the people who had been there to speak and they were her peers and colleagues. All she really remembered about it was how much she had wanted to get the hell out of there. But if she had left an impression on at least one mind then she supposed it was worth it.

"Yes, I do remember that lecture." Devon turned and continued up the hill. She took a little satisfaction when she heard Steve grunt as he pushed himself from the tree. It wasn't like her to be so bitchy, but she really hated pricks like him who automatically assumed that they knew best, mostly because they were men. Exactly the kind of guy who didn't take a polite *no* from a woman they found attractive.

Angela continued to prattle on about the lecture and everything she remembered about it and how much she respected what Devon had said. Devon occasionally expressed appreciation at the young woman's compliments.

As the trail leveled out a few yards from the rangers' cabin Steve fell into step with Angela again and his labored breathing began to ease. He still wasn't very talkative but at least he didn't sound like he was going to hyperventilate anymore.

Devon breathed a sigh of relief when she saw the forestry truck housed under the building. They made their way around the opposite side and Devon knocked. It took just a moment for Elaine to open the door but it seemed like an eternity as Devon anticipated seeing the ranger again. She was wearing faded jeans and a long-sleeved Mount Hood T-shirt that molded to her breasts. Devon glanced down and wanted to burst out laughing at the slippers on her feet but somehow managed to hold it in. She would have never pegged Elaine for the fuzzy bear slipper kind of woman but it was absolutely adorable.

"Hi." Elaine was noticeably surprised to see Devon at the doorstep of her cabin.

It took Devon a moment to find her voice.

"These two seem to be off course." Devon indicated over her shoulder to the pair standing behind her.

Elaine stood back and held the door open. "Come on in."

When everyone was inside Elaine looked at Devon. "How is it you came to bring these two to my door?"

Devon rolled her eyes. She really didn't want to get into this; she just wanted to head back down the mountain. "Steve here was trying to fill his canteen from a small side pool in the river across from where I was working."

Elaine glanced at him in alarm. "You haven't drunk from that river before have you?"

"No. We had just come up to it. My canteen was empty so I was going to refill it." He glared at Devon. "Until she threw a rock at me."

Elaine appeared to be struggling to suppress her smile. "You should be damn thankful that she did. May I please see both of your driver's licenses?"

"My license? For what? She threw the rock at me!"

"Yes, sir, I'm sure she did. But she did it to save your life. You on the other hand were in an unauthorized area of the forest. There are signs clearly posted on all of the *approved* trails and had you been paying attention you wouldn't have been in a restricted zone."

"But she was there." He pointed his finger at Devon.

For a man who stood well over six-feet-tall he acted like a three-year-old. Devon was enjoying Elaine's handling of the situation.

Elaine shrugged. "She is supposed to be there. She works for the federal government. You do not. So, your license?"

Angela smacked Steve on the chest as she handed Elaine her license. "Oh, for God's sake just give it to her. If you had listened to me in the first place we wouldn't be here. I'm sorry. We started out on an approved trail, but thanks to Steve, somehow we ended up here."

As Steve finally pulled his license from his wallet, he shot a look of annoyance at his girlfriend. Devon was surprised to see Elaine actually write them both a ticket, but then again she did have a job to do and wouldn't be much of a ranger if she didn't make sure people adhered to the posted laws. Once she was done writing the citations, she returned their licenses and requested they sign the tickets.

"Where are you heading?"

Angela studied the topographical map on the wall. She pointed to a ridge that ran along the river in the next valley. She gave Steve a withering look before she turned back to Elaine. "We're supposed to be here." She pointed to a location on the map. "I was told it was within a day's hike of Top Hat Lake. We were going to meet some friends up there for a couple of days and then hike out."

"This early in the season?"

Angela nodded her head. "We packed plenty of cold weather gear. We were just going to do some research for an advanced wildlife biology class we are taking this summer. Dr. Langford said that it would help and he said one of his colleagues did it all the time." Angela turned toward Devon. "I guess he meant you, Dr. McKinney."

"And you are both in this class?" Elaine asked with an arched eyebrow.

"Just me. Steve is my boyfriend. He thought he should come along just in case."

Devon and Elaine shot each other looks. *Oh brother!* Devon

made a mental note to talk to Dr. Langford when she got back about sending his students out so early.

"Why don't you two wait outside for a moment? I need to talk to Dr. McKinney and then I'll take you over to the Northridge trail and you will be within a couple hours of the lake."

"Thank you." Angela grabbed Steve by the hand and dragged him out of the cabin.

Once the door was closed Elaine indicated that Devon should sit down on the couch. Elaine took the other end next to a pair of well worn Doc Martens and a pair of socks.

"Thanks for taking the time to bring them up here. God only knows what kind of trouble those two could have gotten themselves into. Especially since they weren't even headed in the right direction and I still have poachers up here."

Devon was trying mightily not to smile as Elaine kicked off her adorable slippers and pulled on socks. "Do you think they'll be all right up at the lake?"

"Yeah. They should be fine." Elaine began lacing up one of her boots. "Does your doctor friend often send his students up here?"

Devon shook her head. "This is the first I heard of it. But when I get back I plan to talk to him about it."

Elaine nodded. "Good. How much time will you lose for your research?"

Devon looked at her watch again. "I should make it back down the mountain just as the sun sets. This should only set me back a day."

"I'll be down to help you out tomorrow."

"That really isn't necessary, Captain. But I appreciate the offer."

They both stood as Elaine adjusted her pant legs over her boots. Devon had an unobstructed view of her ass. She tried not to look and completely failed. It should be illegal for anyone to fill out denim that well.

Hoping to avoid being caught staring, she readjusted her ball

48

cap. "I guess I better get going if I'm going to make it back down before the light fades."

"Be careful and I'll see you tomorrow." Elaine smiled, ignoring Devon's insistence that she need not help her with her research. Elaine's smile took her breath away and Devon wondered how someone she had just met could have such an effect on her.

Devon was exiting the cabin when she replied, "Okay, but it still isn't necessary for you to come down."

She shook her head as she passed Steve and Angela who were still bickering over their location and who would pay for the tickets. Devon said a polite but quick "goodbye" to Angela and hurriedly picked up the deer trail that would lead her back to camp. She may have lost a day's work but she was incredibly thankful to be rid of those two. That she would see Captain Thomas the following day had nothing to do with the spring in her step.

Chapter 6

Devon awoke earlier than usual to get a timely start. She had to make up the time she had lost the day before while dealing with Angela and Steve. Even though she had told the captain that she need not come down to help her, she had to admit she was hoping that she would, in fact, show up. She hadn't been able to sleep much, her heart unaccountably racing at the recollection of Elaine's silly slippers and well-filled out jeans. It was absurd and a little bit scary. In spite of her reluctance, she couldn't help the smile that formed on her face. *She is one hot ranger!*

She had just finished her morning coffee and was collecting her instruments when she heard the tell tale noises of someone approaching.

"Good morning. Did you get started without me?"

"No, actually, I was just getting ready to head down the river. You're up awfully early, Captain." She ducked her head, afraid that her smile was far too welcoming, or that Elaine would see that she'd just broken out in goose bumps.

"Well, I had a promise to keep. I don't know how much help I'll be. It's not like I have a Ph.D. in botany. But I am at your disposal, Dr. McKinney."

God, she has a beautiful smile. "Today I am going to concentrate on collecting samples along the bank about two hundred yards downstream. Think you can handle that, Captain?" Devon couldn't prevent the smirk that followed her playful sarcasm. Better to emphasize a little professional rivalry than stand there blushing like a teenager.

"Hmmm. Not sure, but I'll do the best I can. You teach and I'll learn, how's that?"

"Sounds like a deal." She gestured to a knapsack lying on the ground, an unspoken request for Elaine to carry it, as she grabbed another and motioned for Elaine to follow. For some reason she was vividly recalling that Elaine had seen her naked while she skinny-dipped. A few days ago she hadn't been embarrassed, but now she found herself wondering if Elaine was recalling it too.

Thankfully, it didn't take them long to reach their destination. Devon knew she would settle down as soon as she was working. She kept her instructions brief and Elaine was an apt pupil. They spoke little, except for the occasional question and answer regarding the collection process.

It was obvious to Elaine that when Devon was working she was entirely focused. She couldn't keep herself from watching Devon as she worked so intently, stealing glances when she was confident she wouldn't be caught. With each glance, she found the woman more and more attractive and intriguing and couldn't help but be reminded of seeing her nude. It had surprised her when Devon had taken the situation so lightly. Was it possible that Devon had enjoyed being watched?

Time seemed to fly and soon it was mid-afternoon. Stretching her back and flexing her arms, Devon hoped she sounded casual as she said, "We've done enough for today. Besides it feels like the weather's changing."

As Elaine tried to stand, she lost her balance. Devon quickly clutched her hand, holding her until she regained her footing. At the mere touch of Devon's skin against her own, Elaine was certain that electricity had shot up her arm and the impression of the woman's hand was burned forever on her skin. Her breath caught in her throat and she had felt like her heart would thump painfully out of her chest.

"Thank you." Elaine managed, in an effort to hide her embarrassment and arousal.

Once safely on her feet, she actively tried to look anywhere but at Devon's breasts. For the first time she realized just how sore she was. She suddenly felt like a senior citizen in serious need of a walker. *How on earth does she do this work day after day?*

"Thank you for your help. I think we managed to make up for the lost time. If you'd like we could head back to my campsite and grab something to eat?" Don't blush, Devon thought. It's not as if you just asked her out on a date.

"Sounds good. You're the boss. Today anyway." Elaine laughed and Devon couldn't help but join in.

"I agree with you. The temperature does seem to be dropping pretty rapidly. The storm is well on its way."

"Yeah, but I'm ready for it. I made sure to bring my cold weather gear, so I'll be fine."

It wasn't long before they made it back to camp where Devon offered her meager hospitality.

"Unfortunately, all I have are packaged meals and protein bars."

"A protein bar sounds great. I'm starving. I nearly got worked to death today."

"Yeah, right. For a tough ranger you sure can whine." Devon flashed her a playful grin.

As Devon stirred about the campsite, Elaine watched in

amazement at how gracefully she moved. She had thought once or twice that out of the corner of her eye she had seen Devon looking her way. Was Devon interested? Elaine quickly disregarded the thought as her own wishful thinking.

She was afraid she had been caught staring again as Devon suddenly turned and approached her with two bottles of water and a couple of protein bars. If she'd noticed, she didn't give Elaine any indication. Along with her other qualities, Devon always seemed to be the consummate professional. Elaine had been berating herself for her own lack ever since she laid eyes on Devon. She was usually very professional, but around Devon, she was more like a clumsy teenager.

After graciously accepting the snack from Devon, she devoured it and then chugged the bottle of water.

"Before I head out, I wanted to say that I had a good time today."

"A good time? Crouched on the ground, freezing your ass off, that's a good time?" Devon smiled, trying to make light of the compliment.

Elaine smiled sheepishly, almost embarrassed at how asinine the comment sounded. "What I meant to say is it was nice spending time with you today."

"Likewise. And I truly do appreciate your help."

"My pleasure. After all, it was those geographically challenged hikers who held up your work yesterday. And they were my problem, not yours."

They stood motionless in silence for a moment.

Elaine knew she should simply say goodbye and return to the cabin, but her feet wouldn't move.

Their eyes locked for the briefest of moments before Devon turned away, afraid not only of what she saw in Elaine's eyes, but also afraid of what her own eyes might reflect. When she met Elaine's eyes again she was helpless to break free. She hadn't been close enough before to truly appreciate just how dark and beautiful Elaine's eyes were. She could feel the heat from Elaine's body and her knees became inexplicably weak.

Devon had no idea who was actually moving, only that the space between them was narrowing. She only knew that those lips that she'd been studying all day were coming closer. Her own lips parted slightly and Devon couldn't quite stifle her gasp. She realized that Elaine looked confused and scared—just the way Devon felt.

The first touch of Elaine's lips was tentative. As Elaine's lips returned more firmly, Devon couldn't stop the moan that escaped her as she opened her mouth inviting Elaine's tongue in.

Elaine's hunger grew as she took possession of Devon's mouth. All shyness fled as they tasted each other. Her hand found its way under Devon's sweatshirt to caress the soft flesh of her back as their kiss deepened.

Devon felt Elaine's strong arms embrace her as she reached up and ran her fingers through Elaine's hair, surprised at how soft it felt between her fingers. Devon had been kissed before, but never like this.

They finally parted and each tried to catch their breath. Elaine continued to stroke the softness under her hand. She couldn't seem to release Devon. "I'm sorry. I didn't mean to do that."

Devon was shocked at how low and sultry her voice was. Her eyes felt heavy lidded. "*Are* you sorry?"

Elaine groaned and pulled Devon tighter against her as she fiercely reclaimed her soft, sweet mouth. Her hands stroked Devon's ribs and then slipped easily upward, seeking out the silk covering her breast. The pleasure and arousal was overwhelming as she pulled away to look into Devon's eyes once more.

Devon hungrily pulled Elaine back to her again for another kiss. Surprised at her own aggression, she stroked her tongue against Elaine's, first firmly and then playfully suggesting just how talented and agile it would be on other parts of her body. Had she ever been this aroused, this wet, from a kiss?

Elaine finally managed to release Devon. She stepped back,

trying to look like she had some semblance of control. *What the hell just happened?* "I guess I should be going. I have ranger duties to attend to. Be careful and have a safe night. If you need me, you know where to find me."

Devon's lips were swollen and the ache between her thighs begged for release. She could still feel the heat from Elaine's hands on her body. She knew that if the kiss had continued she would not have been able to stop herself from giving into the passion she felt. The word "no" would not have been anywhere in her vocabulary. Now Elaine was strolling off as if nothing of import had happened. She stepped out of Devon's arms as quickly as she stepped into them and with ease it seemed.

Elaine disappeared into the forest without a backward glance. *One thing is for sure, that woman can kiss!* Devon stood there for a while longer trying to steady her weak legs, ultimately deciding that if she threw herself back into her work she might be able to forget about what had just happened. *Yeah right!*

Chapter 7

By the time Elaine reached her cabin it was clear the predicted snowstorm was going to be a reality. Late season snow could be some of the most hazardous—quick, wet and far colder than people were prepared for. She got the latest report from Brad, who had been getting regular updates from the National Weather Service. Rapidly falling temperatures overnight, flurries by midday and heavier snowfall by early evening that could last from thirty-six to forty-eight hours. After sharing a few administrative details, she thanked Brad for the report and went out on the deck. It was cold and she pulled her jacket closed around her.

The sky was clear and the stars were out. She shivered slightly. She didn't really believe that it was just the night air giving her the chills. She wanted to see Devon again. She wasn't sure what had caused her to lose her inhibitions and kiss her, but now she was unsure as to what to say or do when she saw Devon next. It hadn't all been one-sided. Devon had definitely kissed her back.

She sighed, watching her breath form clouds in the air. Yes, she wanted to see Devon again, but she wasn't sure it would be a good idea. She needed to warn Devon that the approaching snow would probably be worse than she anticipated. She had made it clear that she was expecting the storm and was prepared for it, but Elaine couldn't in good conscience ignore her duties because of personal reasons—reasons she created. On the heels of that thought was the realization that Devon might pack it in and head home after considering how the likely snow levels would hamper her work for the next week. She didn't want to consider why that thought was so unsettling.

The following afternoon, Elaine leaned against a tree, silently watching as Devon worked. She knew that she probably should have alerted Devon to her presence immediately, but she couldn't bring herself to say anything. Devon was bent over foliage, taking photographs. Her jeans clung to her body perfectly. When she stood up, Elaine's mouth went dry at the sight of the fleece molding to Devon's breasts. She was thankful for the tree's support.

Devon had felt the change in temperature, but ignored it as she photographed the brush growing on the river bank. She had a few more minutes of good light before shade once again spread over the foliage and she needed to take as many shots as possible.

She had just packed her belongings and turned to head back to her camp when she saw Elaine standing there, a slow smile spreading across her face.

Good God, the ranger moved quietly.

"Good afternoon," was all Elaine could think to say.

The look in her eyes set Devon's body ablaze instantly.

"I wanted to let you know that the snowstorm is expected to come in this evening. It will be bitter cold tonight and the snowfall will begin tomorrow. The report suggests moderate to heavy accumulation; probably twelve inches or more. You don't have much time if you want to pack out of here."

Devon looked at her in surprise, shock almost. "No. I have work to do. I won't be leaving." Devon attempted to mask her irritation at Elaine's assumption that a little snow would drive her from camp by giving her a slight smile. *Just what kind of a wimp does she think I am?* She wasn't some delicate flower that would wither and die when faced with some inclement weather.

She couldn't prevent the mischievous smile that spread across her face as she said a little more sarcastically than she had intended, "You're welcome to leave, Captain. You don't have to stay up here on my account."

Elaine smiled. "I'm not worried about me. I'm the one with the warm cabin remember?"

Devon couldn't help but laugh. "True enough." Devon enjoyed Elaine's sense of humor but she wasn't going to be one-upped. "I guess I'll have to dig out my snow boots. Besides, I'm always prepared. As I told you before, I brought my cold weather gear. I thought I might encounter snow at some point so I brought plenty of warm clothes and my sleeping bag is rated to forty below. Don't worry about me, I'll be perfectly fine."

Elaine felt like someone else was controlling her as she heard herself say, "Well, if you are planning to stay, perhaps you should come up to the cabin with me. I can offer you a warm, safe place to stay until the snow passes."

Devon briefly wondered how spending time alone snowbound with Elaine could possibly be safe. Her body trembled as she considered all the ways Elaine could keep her warm.

"Well?" Elaine asked.

"That won't be necessary. I should be fine. But thank you for the offer."

Elaine knew that she had done her job by updating Devon about the storm. She had even offered her a warm place to stay. Elaine knew she should turn around and walk away, but her feet felt like lead weights. For some reason, even though she had no reason to assume Devon was anything but capable, she couldn't bear the thought of her braving the storm and the cold alone in the woods.

"I'm sorry, Dr. McKinney, but my job is to keep these woods and everyone in them safe."

Devon knew that it wasn't really necessary for her to leave her camp and she wanted to be irritated with Elaine's tone, but those eyes hypnotized her, making her forget all the reasons why she shouldn't go. "All right, just let me grab a few things."

When Devon turned away Elaine silently shook her head. What was she thinking? Jesus, how was she going to spend the night in such close quarters with the woman that she was so incredibly attracted to?

Elaine couldn't help but notice how Devon moved with such poise and how at ease she was in this environment. She watched as Devon gathered some clothes, her toothbrush, toothpaste, lotion and her laptop, complete with a spare battery. She shoved everything in a small pack. Before leaving, Devon gathered up things around her camp, including a lantern and a strange looking grate that she pulled off the fire pit and placed them in her tent. When she had finished, she zipped the fly door closed and stood in front of Elaine ready to leave.

Elaine glanced at the tent and decided that it should be fine. It was made to endure the weather and wind. When Devon had said that she would be fine, she wasn't kidding. Still Elaine would feel better knowing that Devon wasn't out in the freezing temperature. She also admitted to herself that it wasn't the only reason she wanted Devon with her in the cabin. *Jesus.*

Elaine was quiet as she led Devon up the hill.

Devon never had any trouble keeping up. She took the rocks and fallen trees with ease and was careful not to step on any plants.

They followed the deer trail almost to the access road and then broke off to finish the hike to the cabin. Elaine showed

Devon in and busied herself lighting a fire in the fireplace.

"I'll be right back. I need to go start the generator and get some more wood."

"Is there anything I can do to help?"

Elaine smiled. "No, I'll just be a minute. Make yourself comfortable. Feel free to use the shower—all the facilities. I know you've probably missed them."

"Oh, a shower would be great. Thanks." Devon picked up her pack and promptly disappeared into the bathroom with an eager grin.

They had made it back just as the clouds began moving in and the temperature plummeted. She carried in a full armload of wood, then busied herself with oil lamps and the beginning preparations of chili. The light frost on the windows obscured her view of the valley and once again she was thankful they had made it back when they had. She ignored the sounds from the shower, but try as she might she couldn't help but imagine Devon, the way she'd looked skinny-dipping, now only few feet away, on the other side of a door...

It was going to be a long night.

The water on her skin felt good and it was the first time Devon had truly felt warm since arriving in the Cascades. Her solar shower usually did an adequate job, but having a genuine hot shower was blissful. She finally felt clean.

It was nice to stand in a warm body and slather lotion over her dry skin. The cabin had been heating up nicely when she entered the bathroom so she had chosen a pair of loose fitting boxer shorts and a T-shirt to sleep in. The thought of wearing clothes to bed wasn't appealing, but the luxuries that the small cabin afforded were worth it.

She finally emerged from the bathroom with brush in hand. She was still brushing her hair out when her stomach grumbled.

The smell of food filling the room made her realize for the first time that she hadn't eaten anything except a breakfast bar at mid-morning.

Elaine looked up just as Devon emerged from the bathroom and her breath caught. How on earth was she supposed to get through dinner much less the night with Devon dressed like that? The shirt was old and worn and molded perfectly to Devon's firm breasts. And those legs! Jesus, they had haunted Elaine's dreams. She had so many visions of them wrapped around her body and now they would be within just a few feet of her. She was torn between wanting to beg Devon to put on more clothes and wanting to rip off what little she was wearing.

She finally found her voice. "I didn't know if you like chili, if you do, dinner is ready. If not, I'd be happy to make you something else."

Devon smiled. "Chili sounds great, much more appetizing than my typical dinners when I'm working. I don't know how they have the audacity to call those freeze dried meals *food*. Thank you for saving me from another one of those."

Elaine finally tore her gaze away. "It's no problem. What can I get you to drink?"

"Whatever you're having will be fine?"

"Beer?"

Devon grinned. "That sounds great."

Devon filled the two bowls that Elaine had set out with steaming chili while Elaine grabbed spoons, napkins and two beers from the refrigerator and brought them to the table. Devon blew on a spoonful making sure it wouldn't burn her mouth. For chili that had been quickly thrown together it was good, with a nice spicy kick that Devon enjoyed.

"This is really good, Captain."

Elaine's eyes reflected her appreciation of the compliment. "I'm glad you like it." She couldn't even begin to understand why the word "Captain" rolling off of Devon's tongue made her whole body quiver. As much as she enjoyed the sound of it, she decided it was much too official.

"Dr. McKinney, you don't have to be quite so formal. You are welcome to call me Elaine, you know?"

"Okay, Elaine, but only if you call me Devon. And please do. I never quite get used to being called *Dr.* McKinney."

Elaine knew she should address the kiss at some point. She sat quietly pondering how to approach the subject. Finally, she muttered, "Um, about yesterday. I'm sorry for kissing you. I don't know what got into me. I hope you will forgive my impulsiveness."

Devon, even more confused than before, didn't know what to say. "Okay. Well, let's just chalk it up to a lapse in judgment. On both our parts. Fair enough?"

Elaine nodded, glad that neither wanted to make a federal case out of it. She knew deep down that it wouldn't be that easy to put it behind them, but at least they had acknowledged it. She decided work was the safest topic. "How are the samples looking?"

Devon was well aware that botany bored most people, even forest rangers. But as they ate, Elaine continued to ask questions that showed she was not only listening, but was actually interested. Devon found herself telling Elaine everything about the tests she had taken right after the spill and the results of what she was currently working on.

They shared stories of their personal experiences during the spill, both agreeing that they had obviously not met during that time.

Their conversation began to gravitate from work to their personal lives. They exchanged stories about how they had gotten into their respective professions and neither noticed when the snow began to fall.

"How long have you been a ranger?"

Elaine mentally counted. "It has been fourteen years now, I guess."

"How long have you been captain?"

Elaine smiled as she reflected on her career, "About three

years. I would probably be further along if I could bring myself to play politics."

Devon returned her smile. "Why, Captain Thomas, I would not have pictured you as a rebel."

"This coming from a rogue botanist!"

Devon's smile widened and she shrugged. "I can't say I particularly like the politics myself."

Elaine arched an eyebrow. "I'm sure you are far better with it than I am."

"Probably, but you chose a profession where you are out in the field. You are out there every day." Devon gestured toward the mountains beyond the windows. "You spend your days in the forests. I've had to earn that right. I've always been good at research, tucked away in the lab and I've always loved plants. So it made sense for me to become a botanist, but it has been difficult for me to prove that I need to be where I can do the most good. And sometimes, well, a lot of times, that's in the field."

Elaine nodded in understanding. She went to the fridge to get them each another beer. She opened a bottle and set it in front of Devon, who hadn't been shy about getting a second helping of dinner. Elaine wasn't sure if Devon just enjoyed the chili because it wasn't freeze dried or if she actually liked it. Either way, Elaine was glad to see Devon indulging in another bowl.

Several hours later, after the dishes had long been washed and the fire was burning low, Elaine headed for the bathroom in her stocking feet to take a shower. Alone for the first time, Devon studied the cabin. The room was small, but cozy. Or perhaps Devon found the cabin comfortable because of the company. It had been a long time since she was able to talk to someone other than her family or co-workers about her job. The more they talked the more Devon realized that they shared common interests and the conversation was genuine and comfortable.

Maybe Elaine wasn't a puzzle after all, but then again, what was with her kissing and running? And then apologizing?

Several minutes later Elaine emerged from the bathroom. She was wearing boxer shorts and a tank top. Not surprisingly, she was incredibly fit. Devon couldn't help but notice her strong stomach visible beneath the ribbed tank top. Her legs were equally muscular as were her arms. She could barely smother a laugh when she noticed the prominent tan lines midway between her elbow and shoulder. They were clearly a result of the many hours she had spent in the sun wearing her uniform. Her entire body, silhouetted by the fire was divinely feminine.

Elaine seemed lost in thought as she towel dried her hair in front of the fire and sifted the long auburn locks through her fingers. The dancing flames highlighted the hints of gold that had been previously concealed in a thick braid. Devon was thankful for the dim lighting as her face grew heated and without a doubt flushed, at the sight of Elaine's body. She was embarrassed when she noticed that Elaine had caught her looking.

"Do you want me to put some extra blankets on the bed or will you be warm enough?"

"If I take the bed where are you going to sleep? No offense, but this couch doesn't seem like it would be particularly comfortable for sleeping."

Elaine shrugged. "It's probably not the most comfortable, but it will be fine."

"You were kind enough to share your cabin, so you should take the bed." Devon didn't relish the idea of sleeping on an uncomfortable couch or the floor, but she would. It certainly wouldn't be any worse than sleeping in her sleeping bag.

"No, Devon, you're a guest and this is my job. You take the bed, I'll take the couch. It'll be fine."

Devon, not wanting to argue any further, reluctantly agreed. She watched as Elaine collected a pillow, sheet and quilt from the built-in cabinets across from the bed.

Elaine threw a few more logs onto the fire to ensure the fire would warm them throughout the night.

Once the couch was prepped, they climbed into their respective beds for the night. Bidding each other goodnight, Devon settled deeper under the covers. The sheets still held Elaine's scent and like a Pavlovian reaction, a dull throb began between her legs. The thought of being in Elaine's bed had tantalized the peripherals of her imagination over the last several days. Now she was here, not under the circumstances she had fantasized about and her mind wouldn't still as she lay listening to the crackling of the fire thinking about how much nicer it would be if Elaine's arms were wrapped around her. She rolled over trying to quell the ache that built inside of her as well as her rampant wayward mind. She desperately hoped sleep would claim her soon and release her from her self-imposed torment.

Chapter 8

Elaine awoke first, thanks to the frigid temperature. The fire had consumed the logs during the night and the quilt she had counted on to keep her warm wasn't sufficient without the warmth of the fireplace. As quietly as possible, so as not to wake Devon, she dressed and slipped outside the cabin to gather more firewood, cursing herself for not being more thorough the night before.

Distracted, much? She had only herself to blame. She knew once she had a fire going, it would take little time to warm the cabin to a comfortable temperature.

Once outside she was surprised to find that the snow had begun sooner and at a much heavier rate than had been predicted. Over a foot had already accumulated on the ground. She gathered as much wood as her arms could hold and headed up the snow-covered stairs into the cabin. She fumbled with the doorknob trying to open the door without dropping any of the logs she held. Just as she managed to open the door, she felt herself sliding. Within seconds, not only was all the wood she had been carrying on the cabin floor, but so was she, flat on her ass.

Devon flew out of bed, noticeably startled. "Oh my God! What happened? Are you okay?"

"I'm so sorry. I didn't mean to wake you. I just went out to get some firewood and as you can see, busted my ass on the way in."

"Why didn't you wake me for heaven's sake? I could have helped, you know?"

"There was no reason for us both to freeze our asses off."

Devon all but rolled her eyes as she stood over Elaine, hands on hips. "Well, let me help you up. Are you hurt?"

"No, I'm fine. A little embarrassed, but fine."

"You are you sure you're okay?" Devon asked skeptically.

"I'll get a fire started and then make some coffee. How does that sound?"

"Heavenly, nothing better than a nice cup of coffee after being woken up with the thought that the walls are caving in around you."

"Yeah, sorry about that."

Devon waved off her words. "No need to apologize. I'm just glad you didn't hurt yourself."

Just my pride. Elaine rubbed her backside as she continued stacking logs in the fireplace. "There is quite a bit of snow out there. Not sure how much work you will be able to get done today."

"Yeah, I hoped that might not happen, not on this assignment. I always give myself a little extra time on assignments like this just in case bad weather comes my way but it wasn't going to work out this time. But it's March—we could have seventy degrees and blazing sun tomorrow. Why don't you go put on some dry clothes and I'll get the coffee started?"

Elaine nodded in agreement and once the fire was going, she padded off to the bathroom to change into much warmer and dryer clothes. When she emerged, the aroma of coffee had permeated the cabin and the fire had warmed it considerably. Two cups of coffee sat on the kitchen table and Devon was whipping up a quick breakfast.

"Hope you don't mind. Thought I'd make some eggs and toast for breakfast."

"That's perfect, thank you. And again, I'm sorry for waking you."

"Don't worry about it; I would have woken up at some point." They exchanged a quick smile.

As much as she tried, Elaine couldn't tear her gaze away from Devon. She was, by far, the most beautiful woman Elaine had ever seen and the most amazing part was that she doubted that Devon even knew how remarkably attractive she was.

Elaine kept replaying their kiss over and over in her mind, like an old black-and-white movie. Elaine's gaze traveled the full length of her body. Her tongue unconsciously wet her dry lips as her gaze finally settled on Devon's full breasts. It was clear that Devon wore no bra and her erect nipples strained against the shirt that covered them. Elaine felt the now familiar wetness flood her body as she imagined her lips and tongue on Devon's nipples, pulling each one deep into her mouth.

Elaine forced her eyes higher but her breath caught when she saw the slightly parted lush lips that were begging to be kissed. When she finally met the dark gray eyes, she half expected to see irritation at her blatant appraisal. Instead, what she found sent another wave of desire crashing through her. Devon's dark gray eyes were glossy and unfocused and filled with the same carnal desire that Elaine was sure her own eyes reflected.

Elaine quickly looked away, searching for any excuse to escape the moment they had just shared. *Fire, yes, I will stoke the fire.* She rose quickly from the table and headed to the fireplace.

Elaine forced herself to shake off the thoughts. There was no way she would be able to get through the day if she continued to let her mind run rampant this way. She just needed to focus. Just because she and Grace hadn't had sex in what seemed like forever and her attraction to Devon was relentless, that was no reason for her to act like a horny teenager. Not to mention Grace *had* just moved out. It didn't really matter that Elaine had accepted the relationship had been over long ago. There were still very good reasons for her not to get involved with another woman any time soon. But then again Devon McKinney was unlike any other woman she had ever met.

When Elaine could find no other reason not to return to the table, she slowly made her way back to the cup of coffee awaiting her. As she watched Devon stare blankly outside into the pure white wonderland that nature had created overnight, she wondered what she might be thinking. She wondered if perhaps Devon was wishing she was someplace else.

"Are you going to have to postpone your research now?"

Devon turned her gaze from the cabin's front window toward Elaine, but she couldn't bring herself to make eye contact. "No. Once the snow ends, I'll be able to brush it aside and get what I need."

She was relieved by Elaine's question because it shook her from her own musings. She had been staring blindly at the snow wondering why every part of her body longed to feel Elaine's touch. Why had it felt so right when Elaine had pulled her close and kissed her so passionately? Even more importantly, why had Elaine dismissed the kiss so easily, when Devon felt like it awakened in her something she had not felt in a very long time, if ever?

Maybe she was just lonely. Maybe it was the setting, a remote cabin in the woods in the midst of a snowstorm with an extraordinarily gorgeous woman. *Oh God! How cliché is that?*

Deep down she knew that wasn't true. The very first time she had laid eyes on Elaine, she felt her chest constrict and just the sight of the woman had taken her breath away. She had met beautiful women before, but not like Elaine. Most women use makeup to cover their imperfections and highlight their attractive qualities, but Elaine was a natural beauty. She wasn't dressed in designer clothes created to accentuate every curve. She was completely authentic and the most amazing woman Devon had ever seen.

Elaine was far too attractive to be single, if indeed she was. Devon couldn't imagine that there was any woman out there stupid enough to let Elaine get away, unless Elaine wasn't the type to commit to just one woman. That thought disturbed Devon more than it should as did the realization that Elaine better *damn* well be single after laying such an unbelievable kiss on her; a kiss that left her not only throbbing and wet, but weak in more areas than one.

Devon's answer about her research served as a much needed reminder that she was here to work. She had a deadline, her superiors were waiting for her report and she needed to get home to her sister—her very pregnant, very alone sister. She mentally scolded herself for focusing on anything other than work. She had planned ahead, as usual and given herself a little extra time in case of snow, but she would still have to use the time wisely in order to finish on schedule.

So what if Elaine had given her the most remarkable kiss of her life? It didn't matter that Devon could still remember every curve of Elaine's body, or that she could still feel the way her own nipples had swelled in the palm of Elaine's hand. No, there was no reason at all that she should lose sight of her purpose for being up here in these mountains. Unfortunately, all she could think about was why she was in this cabin.

Since there was no way that Devon could actually work while the snow was falling, she chose to spend the day in the warmth of the cabin, taking advantage of the electricity to write out notes and focus on work, though at times it was hard not to simply watch both the snow falling and Elaine catching up on her field reading. If she kept her focus on work after the snow, there was no reason she shouldn't enjoy Elaine's company.

Finally calling it quits on her notes for the day, Devon joined Elaine on the couch in front of the fire.

They talked more about the spill and shared their own personal experiences during the emergency. Devon was grateful for the distraction that the pleasant conversation provided. She learned that Elaine had stubbornly refused to leave her post in spite of the fact that man after man was forced to rotate off the line. Exposure to the toxins and the danger to her crew had been at the forefront of Elaine's mind throughout the cleanup. Despite their hazmat suits, many rangers had fallen ill.

Her respect for Elaine continued to grow, but so did the alarm that Elaine had put her life in jeopardy. There was absolutely no doubt that Elaine was dedicated to both her crew and her job, a quality that Devon understood completely.

"I'm surprised that they let you into the contamination zone so early."

Devon smiled. "I can be very persuasive."

Elaine gave her a look that said she didn't doubt Devon's powers of persuasion, but she still asked, "So how did you get access to the spill site so early?"

"Actually this was the third incident I had worked. Through cooperation with the Forest Service, Park Services, Bureau of Land Management and the Department of Transportation we were finally able to come to an agreement. By having someone dedicated to the environment come in right away, a lot of harm to the plant life and wildlife could be avoided.

"No offense, but rangers are trained in botany. We had to be here anyway. Why not just have one of us handle it? Why expose more people than necessary?"

"If you were fighting a fire, would you stop to take a core

sample of a tree?"

Elaine frowned. "Of course not."

She smiled with satisfaction. "Exactly. You were focused on putting out the fire so to speak. The response crew was focused on their job. There is no way that any one of you would have had time to examine the shrubs and soil when you were busy trying to stop the spread of the pollution."

Elaine's nod seemed to concede the point. "So they let you in. How close did they let you get?"

She knew that Elaine wasn't being condescending. A ranger was trained for every aspect of forest management and during a crisis they didn't like anyone that they considered a "civilian" getting in their way and making things more difficult. Over the years she had learned how to thwart their objections and get the job done.

"I was right there in the thick of it. Smack-dab in the middle so-to-speak."

Elaine's eyes widened. "Only a few select, well-trained crews were allowed that close to the disaster site that early on."

She lifted a brow and asked with amusement, "Do you doubt me?"

Elaine grinned. "No, I don't doubt you. I'm just confused."

"I've been through the training. It was part of a coordinated effort that Congress implemented. I guess they figured if they had more versatile people who were cross-trained to fill multiple roles, they would have to employ less people overall."

"That is the stupidest thing I've ever heard."

"I totally agree, but unfortunately we don't get to make the rules. They do."

Elaine's brow furrowed. "Don't they know how many people would lose their jobs?"

God, she's adorable. "You know how it is. They would rather save a buck than save the environment. That way they have more money to play war."

Elaine's voice rose slightly. "Don't they know that we're

fighting a war out here?"

She placed her hand over Elaine's and said softly, "You don't have to convince me. We both know that they only consider it a war if there are human casualties. The death of our forests and its wildlife, well that's just not important to them in comparison. As far as I'm concerned, preserving our land and wildlife is paramount, but well, the big boys just don't always agree."

The feel of Devon's hand on hers was warm and gentle and strangely comforting to Elaine. She knew that she should probably pull her hand away, but she was loath to do so. Instead she redirected them to the topic they had veered from.

"I guess the Department of Transportation let you into the spill site, because I know the rangers wouldn't have let you in. It was too dangerous."

Devon's laughter filled the room. Elaine loved Devon's laugh.

"I pulled rank."

"What do you mean?"

"Yes, the DOT did let me in and yes, the rangers were against it, but because of my standing with the EPA, they didn't really have much of a choice."

"Aren't you a little young to have such power?"

"How old do you think I am?" Devon's eyes revealed her amusement.

She studied Devon for a long minute. Her skin was flawless, showing no signs of aging or sun damage, even though Devon had told her that she spent a lot of time working in the field. There were laugh lines around her eyes, but that was just evidence of someone who enjoyed life, a trait that Elaine adored.

Okay, so maybe Devon was a genius. "You can't be a day over twenty-five."

Devon chortled. "Don't I wish! I just turned thirty a few months ago."

Elaine, mumbled, "If it makes you feel any better, you're just a baby. I'm thirty-eight."

Devon poked Elaine in the ribs. "That explains a lot."

"What do you mean?"

"Well, *grandma*, I knew there was something I liked about you. I've always had a preference for older women."

"Thanks, I think." She lightly threw a playful elbow in Devon's direction even as she wondered if Devon was serious that she liked older women.

"Seriously, you certainly don't look thirty-eight. I never would have guessed that in a million years. I hope I look as good as you do when I'm thirty-eight."

Not sure what to say, she decided to let the comment slide. "It's impressive that you are held in such high esteem at your age."

"When I was a freshman in college I applied with the EPA. A couple of years later I was offered a job so I finished college early. I was promoted when I got my master's and again when I received my Ph.D. Let's just say, I worked my ass off."

Damn, Elaine was impressed. "To think I thought I was doing good to make captain."

Elaine hadn't realized that she had spoken the words out loud until Devon squeezed her hand. "I am very impressed that you're a captain. I've worked hard to get where I am, but the fact remains that you have far more responsibilities than I do. Not to mention the fact that you are also a woman in a male-dominated field."

She looked into the steel gray eyes and saw the sincerity of Devon's words. "True."

"I study plants, water and soil. I'm not saying that I don't do anything else, or that what I do isn't important, but I don't have nearly as many fields of discipline or training. I don't have to be a firefighter, a police officer or lead a search and rescue team. And let's not forget," Devon added with a wink, "your duties of scaring unsuspecting botanists off of rocks so you can rescue them."

She felt her face flush, partly from her embarrassment, but more from the heat of Devon's hand on hers. *How can a wink and a smile cause me to feel this way?* "So what made you decide to become a botanist, anyway?"

"My mom used to have plants all over the house when we were kids. I used to spend hours with her watering them and talking to them. Every single one of them had a name." Devon's nostalgic smile abruptly faded.

The change in her expression concerned Elaine. "Hey, are you okay?"

"I'm sorry. I hang on to those good memories, but still the reality saddens me."

She waited patiently for Devon to continue.

"I lost my parents while I was in college. That's part of the reason my sister and I are so close. We've always been there for each other and why it is so important that I finish this assignment so I can be home with her when my nephew is born."

"I'm so sorry," she spoke softly as she gave Devon's hand an affectionate squeeze. "If you don't mind my asking, how did it happen?"

"There was a robbery at our house. I guess they thought nobody was home, or maybe they didn't care. Either way, my parents were found in the living room by the police after the neighbor reported gunshots. By the time the paramedics got there, it was too late. I thank God that Raine was out with friends or I would have lost her too. It was hard and I hope that they know the things they taught me as a child made such an impact on me that I chose to do what I do. I'm sorry." Devon paused. "I didn't mean to put a damper on the conversation."

"Not at all." Trying to put Devon at ease, she asked, "What else made you want to be a botanist?"

"My parents used to take us camping every summer. We didn't go to campgrounds or anything like that. We would hike into some remote area and the only things we were allowed to take were the things we could pack in and pack out. I loved it."

Devon looked Elaine directly in the eye and smiled. "It's kind of funny. I'm all about the land and nature and my sister, well; she's a city girl through and through."

Elaine was glad to see Devon's expression clear as she mentioned her sister. There was obviously plenty of affection there.

"Anyway, as the summers passed, more and more people ventured further and further into the woods. I guess I was about eleven when I figured out how disgusted I was by the litter and the disregard people had for nature. We found old tires, refrigerators, oil drums and so many other things that had no reason for being there, other than the callousness of the people who left them there. It was then that I decided that I had to do something to protect the area that I loved so much."

Elaine nodded in agreement. She completely understood where Devon was coming from. She couldn't believe how relaxed she felt talking with Devon. Devon was real and they seemed to share so many of the same thoughts and feelings. She couldn't remember a time that she had shared such an unforced and truly pleasant conversation. It certainly never happened with Grace. Even in the beginning, she and Grace never had much to talk about. Not to mention, Grace didn't have much of a sense of humor, unlike Devon, who seemed not only to love laughing, but made Elaine laugh as well. She and Grace had their passions, but very few in common and Grace had lied about some of hers. It wasn't all bad; it just was what it was.

She was dying to ask Devon more about her home life, precisely if she had someone special at home or if she was single, but instead decided to focus on trying to act like a ranger, not a lust-driven lesbian. After all, she was a professional, right?

"So where do you call home when you're not here in a ranger's cabin?" Devon asked.

"Well, I live in Sandpark Point, but sometimes I feel like I live at the station."

"How funny, I live in Barrington. I go to Marblerock all the time to shop. I'm surprised we've never met before now or at least seen each other."

A moment of silence passed before Elaine glanced up at Devon again and suddenly the site of wet, perfectly tanned skin glistening in the sun flashed before her eyes. *Yep, way to be a professional, El.* Trying to ignore the rise in her body temperature, she stumbled for the first time during their conversation, searching for words. She had been curious about something ever since she had seen Devon swimming in the pool. "So, is there a story behind the tattoo I noticed on your shoulder or is it just a youthful indiscretion?"

"That goes back to college. A few months after my parents died I decided to get it as a reminder. It's a phoenix rising from the ashes. It was a moment of clarity and commitment and a constant reminder that I can survive anything."

Devon paused as though lost in thought before asking, "So what about you? What made you decide to become a ranger?"

Elaine smiled as she realized how similar her story was to Devon's. "My parents used to send me to summer camp. I hated it there because I never seemed to fit in. It was hard to go to camp and bunk with a bunch of girls knowing that I was different. I wanted to be *with* the girls, but I didn't want to be with the girls talking about boys."

She shrugged before continuing. "So I would take long walks in the woods. That's how I met my first girlfriend and figured out exactly why and how I was different."

Devon laughed. "Ah, so it was a woman who got you into forestry?"

"Not really, she just happened to be there. We did use the woods as a haven to learn things the camp counselors didn't teach," she said with a flirtatious wink. "But it was in those same woods that she eventually broke up with me."

Devon gave a sympathetic nod.

"Anyway, one summer I was out hiking and I found an injured bird tangled up in the woods. It had tried to use the plastic ring from a six-pack to make its nest. The poor thing had been struggling so hard to get out that it broke its wing. I took it back to the bunkhouse and kept it in a box. The other girls thought I was a freak for touching the bird and mocked me relentlessly, but I just couldn't stand to see it hurt. I was afraid that if I didn't help the poor thing, it would die."

"They're the freaks. How can anyone let an innocent creature suffer?"

Elaine could feel Devon's empathy and it didn't help her promise to remain professional. "After I found the bird, I started reading a lot about the animals indigenous to the area and their natural environment. As I looked around, I realized what we were doing to the earth. Our counselors would just find a tree, bury their ax in it and never give it a second thought. They never even considered the dangers of campfires on hot, dry summer nights. So I continued to read and began resenting the people who were supposed to be teaching me." Elaine smiled playfully. "I guess that's when I became a rebellious protester. And quit going to summer camp too."

"So what happened with the bird?"

"I made a splint using a Popsicle stick for its injured wing. It seemed like in no time at all, it was ready to return to its home. So I took it back into the woods and let it go."

"And you've been taking care of animals ever since."

Elaine nodded. "I try. Then something stupid like this fucking train wreck happens, not to mention these damn poachers and I wonder if I'm doing any good at all."

"Of course you are. You obviously take your work seriously. We both do. The reason we both get so pissed off is because we both care so much."

Elaine definitely had to agree with that logic.

"May I ask you another question?" Devon felt reluctant, but wanted to know.

"Sure."

"The entire time we've been talking, you haven't mentioned

anything about your family or friends. I guess I'm curious."

Elaine paused for a long moment, gathering her thoughts. "Well, there's not much to tell, really. My parents were pretty good when I was growing up. Normal parents as far as parents go, I guess. But that changed when I came out."

She blew out a long breath. "I was a teenager when I came out and at first my father acted like I was just being defiant and then he just acted like an ostrich… He stuck his head in the sand and pretended like it never happened. If he didn't acknowledge it, it wasn't real. As far as my mom goes, she just couldn't accept who I was and tried relentlessly to turn me into the daughter she wanted rather than the daughter she had." Her short laugh had no humor in it.

"My mom was always trying to get me to date the neighbor's son, or trying to set me up on blind dates with young men that her friends knew. She played canasta once a week with her club. Every single week, without fail, it seemed that one of the women had found me the perfect boy, or so they'd say. It was kind of funny. No matter how many times I told her, she just didn't hear me. But in their eyes, they still had a chance to get it right with my brother, Brody. He's seven years younger than me. Because of our age difference, it didn't really affect him at the time. When he was finally old enough to understand, it didn't matter to him one way or the other. He was always the center of his own universe and became the center of my mom and dad's as soon as I came out."

"Where is your family now?"

"My dad retired about four years ago. He was a welder on oil pipelines. I guess they were tired of the Pacific Northwest so they moved to Florida. How cliché, huh?"

"What about your brother? Where is he?"

"Brody went with them to Florida. He's never been what I would consider motivated. I guess after I came out, they did everything they could to make sure he turned out better than I did, in their eyes, anyway."

Devon didn't try to disguise her anger, "That's bullshit! Elaine, being gay doesn't mean there's anything wrong with you! It's your family's loss."

Elaine smiled, "Well, it doesn't seem like my parents did my brother any favors. He has no education and no ambition. He's thirty-one years old and still lives at home with them. He spends most of his days surfing and works part-time at a beach bar. My parents are proud of him. As far as my parents are concerned, at least he's not gay and that makes him damn near perfect."

"Do you see them or talk to them often?"

"No, I haven't seen them at all since they moved to Florida. We've spoken maybe twice since they moved and both times I had to call them. The conversation was strained to say the least. It's kind of like an unspoken don't-ask-don't-tell arrangement."

"I'm really sorry, Elaine. If I had known, I never would have asked."

"No, don't be. I dealt with it a long time ago. That doesn't mean that it doesn't still hurt." Elaine smiled proudly. "Besides, the guys in my crew, they *are* my family. There isn't a thing in the world that I wouldn't do for them and them for me. So, it's okay."

"Well nobody should have to deal with their own family treating them that way. You deserve to be appreciated and accepted for who you are."

Their conversation continued, although the subjects weren't nearly as heavy. Devon continued to question Elaine about her life but most of her questions were now centered on her crew.

"How does your sister feel about your work?" Elaine asked, genuinely curious, but also hoping to hear that there was no girlfriend in Devon's life.

"Raine is very supportive, as is my best friend Stacey." She leaned across Elaine to retrieve her laptop. "I have some pictures here. Raine is about seven and a half months pregnant in this picture. It's one of my favorites. She wears the glow of motherhood beautifully."

Elaine recovered from the almost-electrical shock she'd felt as Devon leaned over her and smiled at the affection reflected in Devon's face and voice as she talked about her sister.

"Throughout her pregnancy I think we've become even closer, if that's possible."

"I'm kind of surprised that you are out here when her delivery date is so close."

"Raine is very stubborn. She knows I love my career and told me that if I didn't come out here, she would refuse to let me in the delivery room." Devon's smile grew. "Besides she's in very capable hands. If there is any change in her condition or if she goes into labor, I will be notified immediately."

As she scrolled through the pictures on her laptop describing Raine in various stages of pregnancy, she eventually came to one of Stacey. "This would be the woman to whom my sister's wellbeing is entrusted. She is my best friend Stacey and more like a sister than anything else." Devon laughed. "If you ask Raine she's more like a mother hen. Phillip, Raine's husband, is overseas. He's in the army and although he didn't want to be there when his wife was delivering their son, he didn't have much of a choice. Stacey has already stepped into her role of godmother even though the little guy hasn't arrived yet."

"I think that's great. Um, I should go check the generator and get some more wood," Elaine said abruptly. A crack from the fire was the perfect excuse to get some air. Leaning in to look at photos, the scent of Devon's hair had become too much. Nor should she be so relieved to learn that the object of her desire didn't appear to have someone waiting at home.

She hoped it didn't look like she was running away, but she didn't dare look back at Devon. Fresh air. She needed it badly.

Chapter 9

She blew on her hands as she checked the fuel gauge on the generator. If they got seriously snowed in, she'd be glad of the emergency propane bottles. She had left the cabin so hastily that she had failed to grab her gloves and certainly didn't want to go back inside the cabin to retrieve them.

"Don't be stupid," she mumbled to herself. "So what if she kissed you back? Jesus, your girlfriend just moved out." She laughed bitterly. "Well, your roommate just moved out. You have absolutely no business being interested in that woman. God, what is wrong with you?"

She had just finished locking up the generator and was preparing to load up on firewood when she felt something hit her back. She glanced over her shoulder and realized that she had just been nailed by a snowball. She spun around to see Devon standing not far away. A big smile lit up her face as her laughter echoed through the mountains.

Elaine couldn't help herself, Devon's laughter was infectious and seeing her in her mittens and ski cap, she was just too cute. She completely forgot about the fact that she was *not* here to get involved with a woman. With a deft motion she easily dodged another snowball. Elaine scooped a handful of snow, oblivious to its coldness, quickly packed it into a nice round ball and flung it at Devon, who easily darted aside as she targeted Elaine with another. Elaine immediately felt the wet cold penetrate her clothes as it struck her coat at the top of the zipper, square in the chest.

Devon laughed even harder until Elaine decided that payback was necessary. She attempted to avoid the onslaught of snowballs being hurled at her as she approached Devon. "You are going to pay for that," Elaine threatened playfully.

As Elaine approached Devon employed a different tactic. "I thought a ranger's duty was to protect and serve."

"That's a police officer's motto."

Elaine had a single purpose in mind and when she was close enough, she tackled Devon, burying her in the fluffy wet snow. Devon laughed and half-heartedly tried to push Elaine off her as Elaine scooped up an armful of snow and rubbed it all over Devon.

"Oh my God! That is so cold!" Devon screamed with laughter. She quickly shoved a handful of snow down the back of Elaine's shirt.

Elaine responded by lifting Devon's shirt and spreading snow across her bare stomach.

As Devon squirmed against Elaine's body in an attempt to free herself, Elaine's hand brushed against her breast. Their eyes locked and Elaine's expression quickly changed from playful to provocative. In spite of the cold, Elaine could only feel the heat of Devon's body beneath her, making the numbness of her own body vanish. The darkening of Devon's eyes mimicked that of their brief passionate moment in the woods.

Devon's eyes were captured by a dark obsidian gaze. She realized that Elaine's eyes were brilliant and intense not tainted by gold or brown. They were amazingly dark and turned nearly black with her desire. They were alluring, passionate and drawing Devon closer. She was as helpless to look away from those eyes as she was to stop herself from pulling Elaine's head down for a hungry kiss.

When she felt Elaine's hand move across her abdomen and toward her breast, the kiss deepened. She moaned as Elaine's lips left hers only to return more firmly. Elaine's tongue licked at her lips seeking entry and Devon opened to her. She moaned again as Elaine's tongue slipped into her mouth taking possession.

Elaine was intrigued by the fresh mint that pervaded Devon's mouth. It was the same clean crisp taste that had lingered on Devon's lips before. It was that wonderful flavor that was now filling her mouth as Devon's tongue continued to dance with her own.

Elaine had no idea how long they lay kissing; she only knew that it hadn't been long enough. When they finally parted she realized it had begun to snow again. Her fingers had warmed as they traveled over Devon's body. She had to stop herself before her hands began stripping the clothes that prevented her from feeling Devon's naked breast and she lost total control.

"We better get you out of this snow before you freeze," Elaine mumbled breathlessly.

Devon's eyes glowed as she whispered, "I hadn't noticed."

The snow did nothing to cool her desire as Elaine once again lowered her head seeking Devon's lips. This kiss was long and deep and even more intimate than the first. Elaine forced herself to pull away long enough to catch her breath, but immediately lowered her mouth to Devon's again. She felt powerless to stop kissing Devon, to stop tasting the lips and mouth that had haunted her for so many days.

She heard Devon moan as her weight covered the length of Devon's body. She could feel Devon's mitten-covered hands gently move through her hair as her mouth once again opened. Elaine had no idea where Devon had learned to kiss, but it was sensuous and overwhelming. Elaine knew she was on the verge of losing all restraint until snow falling from a branch in the distance startled her back to reality. She pulled away, trying to regain her composure as she said more firmly than she had intended, "Let's get you inside."

Elaine stood and offered Devon a hand up. She thought for a moment that Devon would refuse her hand, but she finally grasped it allowing herself to be pulled to her feet. The playfulness and passion that had shown in Devon's eyes disappeared as she turned to head back into the cabin, but not before Elaine caught a glimpse of the pain that they now reflected. Elaine wanted to follow, to continue what they had started, but she held back. Instead, she went to gather the abandoned firewood and gather herself.

Way to go, El! Now you've done it. How do you plan on sleeping in the same cabin with her knowing how her body feels under yours and your hands itch to touch her again? And let's not forget about the throbbing between your legs, how do you plan on ignoring that?

They were all good questions and Elaine didn't have any answers.

Devon hadn't planned on starting a snowball fight any more than she had planned on kissing Elaine. She had only wanted to take a few minutes to escape the cabin and get some fresh air. When she had seen the intense look that Elaine still wore, she wanted to lighten Elaine's mood a little. She hadn't even thought about her actions as she pegged Elaine with the snowball.

For a split second she had feared that Elaine would be irritated, but when she turned Devon couldn't help but laugh at the shocked expression on Elaine's face. She had never thought that a snowball fight would turn into unexpected, but intensely passionate kisses. *Damn it, damn it, damn it. What in the hell were you thinking?*

Devon had no idea why Elaine had ended the kiss so abruptly, any more than she knew why Elaine had ended their pleasant conversation and darted from the cabin. The tone of her voice had been sharp and Devon's mind was ravaged with confusion and questions about the change in Elaine's demeanor. And this wasn't the first time. No matter what the reason, she was mystified and couldn't believe that any of the reasons could be good. She thought she had made it perfectly clear that she wanted Elaine. But not only had Elaine ended the kiss, she had instantly pulled away from her. She had tried to read Elaine's eyes, tried to figure out exactly what was going on in her mind, but they revealed nothing; nothing to help her understand how Elaine felt, or why she had withdrawn so suddenly after sharing the most intimate of kisses.

She escaped to the shower before Elaine's return. She didn't want to be in the room when Elaine brought in the firewood. She needed a few minutes alone to gain some perspective and figure out how to conceal her confusion and the pain of yet another rejection. When Elaine had pulled away so unexpectedly, Devon had felt like she had been slapped. She was embarrassed by her wanton display and it had only been her pride that had allowed her to lift her chin, square her shoulders and walk back to the cabin.

Maybe this stubborn woman has been hurt badly. Maybe she has intimacy issues rooted in hurt or fear. She has some thick walls built around her and just when I feel like I'm getting in, she raises them up all over again. But my heart tells me she's worth it.

When Elaine kissed her, she felt helpless to do anything but oblige her passionate instincts. She felt like putty in Elaine's hands. Even her bones felt weakened by the raging fire that Elaine's lips and touch generated in her body. Exploring Elaine's mouth and hearing her moan in pleasure had sent arousal crashing through her body. She didn't want to look at Elaine and recall her soft lips or how her tongue had felt against her own. She didn't want to think about how wonderfully welcome the weight of Elaine's body had been. And she certainly didn't want to remember the way her body had responded when Elaine's hands touched her as she returned the kiss.

She used the time in the shower to decide that she absolutely would not kiss Elaine again. This was the last time she would allow Elaine to kiss her just to suddenly pull away. If Elaine wanted to pretend like it didn't happen or if she felt like it was a mistake, then she would let her. But she would not initiate anymore physical contact. The woman obviously ran hot and cold and she would not set herself up for another rejection.

As the heat of the shower began to warm her she wished that the sun hadn't already set. She would love nothing more than to retreat to her camp, but it was far too dark and dangerous to attempt the hike. Instead, she was forced to face the rest of the night with Elaine. She didn't normally run from difficult situations, but this one seemed impossible. She couldn't forget the instant when Elaine's eyes had darkened with passion. She wondered how in the hell she was going to get through another night.

Finally, as the hot water turned to cold, Devon quit the shower. She took her time drying and moisturizing her body before dressing in her favorite flannel pajama pants and short-sleeved shirt, pulling her hair up into a bun. When there was nothing else to keep her, she exited the bathroom. A fire heated the room as it filled with the aroma of food. Obviously, Elaine had begun cooking dinner. Until that moment Devon hadn't realized how hungry she was. She caught sight of Elaine and had no idea which hunger she needed to satisfy more.

Devon quickly lowered her gaze and said nothing as she pulled her computer onto her lap. She flipped it open and reached into her pack to retrieve her glasses. She continued to dig in her pack until she produced a notebook and a pencil. The notebook sat next to her and the pencil stuck haphazardly in her hair.

She thought briefly about e-mailing Stacey, but her thoughts were much too jumbled. Work would occupy her and that was where her mind really needed to be anyway. She would enter data and once again remind herself that she was here for one purpose, which didn't have anything to do with the woman across the room.

Several minutes later Elaine glanced up to announce that dinner was ready, but the words stuck in her throat. Devon was obviously focused on her work. While making dinner, Elaine had surreptitiously watched her produce one pencil, but now she had three tucked into her hair, one behind her ear and she was chewing on yet another. The glasses accentuated the features of her face and Elaine doubted that she even realized how lovely she was. Everything about the woman was breathtaking.

It had been so hard to pull away, especially since it seemed obvious that Devon hadn't wanted the kiss to end. But Elaine really needed to get some perspective. Whenever she was around Devon she wanted to kiss her and touch her. It began the moment she laid eyes on Devon. The physical attraction had been immediate. But now it was more than that. Having spent time with her, she knew her to be smart, funny, sensitive and caring. And they shared so many of the same interests and passions. She wanted Devon McKinney, in more ways than one. But she had just walked out of one failed relationship. And that was the problem. She wouldn't blame herself for Grace's faults but she did have to look hard at her own shortcomings.

After several attempts, Elaine finally found her voice and announced that dinner was ready. She watched as Devon removed her glasses and rubbed her eyes. She stretched and smiled appreciatively after setting her laptop to the side. As Devon joined her in the kitchen area, Elaine thought again about how wonderful it had been to touch this woman and how hard it was going to be to get through the night.

They sat quietly at the small table eating the beef and vegetable stew that Elaine had prepared. The silence that filled the room was uncomfortable and Devon didn't have a clue how to recapture the relaxed conversation they had shared earlier. Other than the obligatory "thank you" she offered Elaine for the dinner and Elaine's reply, it was dead silent.

Once again she wished that she could escape to her research site and the solitude of her tent. She felt at war with herself. How was she supposed to spend the night trapped on the side of a mountain, feeling miserable? Whatever was bothering Elaine clearly wasn't something she was going to offer up, at least not without some prodding. Devon wasn't the type of person to evade an issue no matter how unsettling. Running away wasn't an option so she decided to face it head-on.

"I'm sorry about what happened outside. If it upset you, that wasn't my intention. I thought the desire was mutual."

Elaine looked shocked. Devon wasn't exactly sure why. Perhaps she wasn't expecting the apology, or maybe she was just startled by the interrupted silence.

"You didn't upset me."

Devon was incredulous. "So you normally go around kissing women and then abruptly pull away without so much as an explanation? Not once, but twice?"

Elaine looked away. She didn't know what to say. She really needed to explain about Grace and that she had just come out of a not-so-good relationship. The problem was that Elaine wasn't sure where to begin. She knew the only way to help Devon understand her hesitation was to share her history and the details of her relationship with Grace, but Elaine wasn't even sure she completely understood the whole thing herself, especially her role in the relationship's continuance when it had fizzled early and obviously wasn't meant to be.

After the silence stretched, Devon decided washing dishes would make more sense than waiting on Elaine. The silent treatment was getting old and she would much rather spend her time working if she was going to be stuck in a cabin with such an infuriating woman.

Elaine watched as Devon returned to the couch and resumed working. She slowly got up from the table and washed her bowl and spoon, the only two items remaining. She returned to the table after snatching a stack of paperwork from the table near the radio and began working her way through it. The air in the room was much too heavy and after achieving very little, she paused, hoping it had been long enough for her to take a hot shower. The water heater was pretty efficient, but there was usually only one person staying at the cabin. She decided to take her chances. She needed the escape.

Just before entering the bathroom she paused. "Devon, I'm sorry." Getting no response she headed in to take her shower. Devon was still working when Elaine finished her shower and exited the bathroom.

"I'm going to be working for a while longer, so if you want the bed tonight, I'd be more than happy to take the couch." Devon's voice was distant, leading Elaine to believe that her apology had done nothing to remedy the tension between them.

"In case you didn't notice last night, the bed is really quite large. It's more than enough room for two, so if you wouldn't mind, we could share the bed. It just makes sense for us to both be comfortable."

Devon studied Elaine for a moment before agreeing. She had no idea how she would manage to sleep, but in spite of her frustration the thought of lying next to Elaine, feeling her body so close to her own, was just too tempting to refuse. She was frustrated, too, at herself for wavering; one moment being receptive to Elaine and the next feeling annoyed and hesitant because of the way Elaine continually withdrew. Devon removed her glasses and unfurled the bun as she ran her fingers through her hair. She smirked as the abundance of pencils that had accumulated in her hair tumbled to the couch. "On second thought, I think I will call it a night as well. My eyes are tired from looking at this screen and I'm starting to see double."

At Elaine's suggestion, Devon took the side of the bed closest to the wall and for the first time she noticed the belt and gun hanging on a hook next to the bed. She had already noticed the rifle Elaine sometimes carried leaning next to the cabin door, but she had never really given much thought to it. Devon was strangely comforted, not only by Elaine's presence, but by the fact that Elaine seemed to instinctively choose the side closest to the door as if to protect her from any intruders.

Elaine double-checked the lock on the cabin door, stoked the fire, added another log and slid under the covers next to Devon, being sure to leave plenty of space between them. Even with the gap separating them, Devon was all too aware of Elaine's body lying next to her. She was certain that she would never be able to fall asleep and was surprised when sleep so easily claimed her.

Equally lulled and disturbed by Devon's deep, steady breathing, Elaine lay awake, deep in thought about the events of the day. She had been upset with herself for not knowing how to explain why she kissed Devon just to pull away…again. She felt like she was in uncharted territory with Devon McKinney and she didn't like it at all. The worst part being that she really enjoyed Devon's company and obviously found her desirable and she didn't want to screw that up. She certainly seemed to be off to a fabulous start with Devon by kissing her and retreating. It was obvious that Devon was pissed. Not that she really blamed her. How could the woman not find her actions confusing? Hell, she found her own actions confusing.

Elaine realized that the ending of her relationship with

Grace had left her with reservations not only about herself but about women in general. She would talk to Devon tomorrow. She would do her best to make her understand.

Elaine rolled over as the morning light peeked through the window. She expected to find Devon next to her or at least on the sofa. Instead, she found an extra blanket on her, the fire stoked and Devon's gear missing from where it had sat by the door. *She must really have wanted to get away from me.* Elaine moved the curtain and verified that while the snow was lighter it was still indeed coming down. She flopped back down on the bed. *Well, fuck!*

Chapter 10

Devon wasn't surprised that it had been days since her return to her camp and there had been no sign of Elaine. As much as it may have hurt, she figured it was just as well. It left her all the more determined to complete her assignment as soon as possible and return home.

The first day back she had made it down the mountain as the snow stopped. It had taken a while and she had gotten very little done beyond digging her tent out and restoring a work area and the fire pit, but she decided that some progress was better than none.

In the days since, she had barely felt the snow or the bite of the cold. And she had done her damndest not to allow thoughts of Captain Elaine Thomas to enter her mind. She focused solely on her research, her nightly reports and her pregnant sister that she needed to get home to.

While she instinctively knew that if Elaine would let her in she would be worth it, she couldn't dwell on that because it seemed that the good captain didn't want the walls around her shattered. It didn't matter that the kisses they shared were amazing. She knew that Elaine wasn't immune to them. She had seen the look in Elaine's eyes and the haze of desire that had filled them. But she was done being rejected by the ranger so instead she threw herself even further into her work and it was paying dividends.

She was up before the sun each morning for breakfast so that when the first rays of light appeared she would be ready to work and she didn't stop until she absolutely had to. On some nights, she worked by the light of her lantern to draw the last soil or core samples. She would eat a quick meal only because she knew she had to, then retire to her tent where she would enter all the data she collected into her computer and wait for the slow process of her Internet to connect so that she could file her reports. She would then send her nightly e-mails to Stacey and Raine before crawling into her sleeping bag to catch a few hours of sleep.

Devon had just spent the last twenty minutes digging through the frozen ground to carefully extract the root of a *vicia gigantean*. It was usually located a little closer to the coast so she was pleasantly surprised to find it. She didn't need to put it under a microscope to see the foam still visible along the roots from the decontaminant that the ground crews had used, but she still slipped it under the field scope to see how the foam was affecting the root structure. Once she charted the root pattern she snapped off a few digital pictures before replanting the root in the ground. Her hands were chapped and beginning to hurt. The long days were taking their toll on her skin but it would all be worth it if she was home with her family sooner than planned.

She had just picked up her gear and was getting ready to pick herself up when someone asked, "Need a hand?"

Devon was so startled she nearly jumped out of her skin. It had been a good week since she had heard that voice. She craned her head around to see Elaine leaning casually against a tree wearing faded blue jeans, a button-down denim shirt, the same

Doc Martens she had seen before and a light fleece jacket with her hair pulled back through a ball cap. She didn't look a thing like a ranger but she looked every bit as sexy as Devon had ever seen her.

Devon looked down at the mud on her hands and pushed herself to her feet. "Umm…I don't want to get mud on you." She turned her hands palms up to show Elaine what she had meant.

Elaine simply shrugged. "Wouldn't have cared."

Devon reached for her water bottle to wash her hands. It was much warmer than washing her hands in the river and it kept her occupied so that she wouldn't have to look at Elaine right away. She was trying to figure out what Elaine was doing here and while she contemplated asking, she decided to wait for Elaine to explain her purpose for the visit.

Elaine cleared her throat as she glanced down at the rock near her foot; she kicked it slightly with the toe of her scuffed boot before meeting Devon's eyes. Watching Elaine's discomfort made her want to take pity on her, but she had promised herself she wouldn't. So she waited patiently for Elaine.

"I know it's the middle of the day and you still have a lot of work to do but I was hoping that maybe you would want to come up to the cabin and have dinner with me. I have a roast on."

Devon cocked her head and regarded her carefully. "You want to have dinner with me?"

Elaine's smile was shy and lopsided. "I thought perhaps we could talk?"

"Talk?"

Once Devon met Elaine's eyes, she knew she had to put herself out there one more time and give Elaine the chance to talk through whatever it was she wanted to talk about.

"I know I owe you an explanation."

Devon looked her straight in the eyes. "Yes."

"Yes to the explanation or yes to dinner."

Devon finally relented and smiled. "Yes to both."

Elaine audibly exhaled and Devon turned before Elaine could

see her grin. "Let me put a few things away and I'll be ready."

Elaine looked at her watch. "It will probably be late…if you…I mean if you would like to stay the night."

Damn this woman was adorable. Devon looked at her for a long moment, trying to discern if there was any other intention behind the invitation. She certainly didn't feel up to any more rejection from this woman. But then again if she didn't put herself in a position to be rejected then it wouldn't be an issue.

"All right. I'll just be a few minutes."

Elaine remained next to the tree as she watched Devon gather her equipment and store it in the tent. There was some brief rustling and a moment later Devon emerged with a daypack that she assumed held Devon's clothes.

She had spent the last week doing patrols and looking for poachers. She had also spent the time trying to figure out exactly what she wanted—no needed—to say to Devon. She knew that she had to apologize to her but it was more than that. She owed Devon an explanation and she had hoped that the words would come to her. They hadn't but she also knew that she couldn't stay away from Devon any longer. There was something about the woman that was like a magnet and Elaine couldn't deny it anymore. So here she was.

She was so nervous. She had thought about how it had felt to sleep next to Devon and she had missed her body. She didn't think that it was possible to sleep next to another woman in a totally platonic fashion and then miss her.

As they made their way up the trail Elaine tried to calm the butterflies in her stomach. It wasn't like they weren't two educated, successful women who couldn't sit down to a meal together.

As they entered the cabin they were greeted by the smell of roasting meat and vegetables and Devon realized how hungry she was.

"If you would like to go ahead and shower while I finish making dinner you're welcome to." Elaine decided to focus foremost on being a good hostess.

"Are you saying I stink, Captain Thomas?"

"No. I just thought you might like a hot shower after all of those…" She turned and saw Devon's smile.

"Relax, Elaine. And yes I would love a shower, but are you sure you don't need any help in here?"

"There isn't much to do, so by the time you get out dinner should be ready."

"All right," she said as she headed for the bathroom.

The table was already set, save for the roast that Elaine was about to put in the center of it when Devon came out. How she managed to put it down without dropping the thing she had no idea. Devon's long hair was still wet and had dampened the very thin cotton material of her well worn T-shirt around her breasts, accentuating them. She also had on a pair of plaid silk sleep pants that accentuated her tight ass and well-defined legs. *Christ, the woman is a goddess.*

Elaine busied herself with uncorking the wine, hoping not to make a complete fool of herself. By some saving grace she managed to remove it without spilling any. As Devon approached the table, Elaine pulled out her chair and it occurred to her that this felt very much like a date. Something she hadn't really done in years.

"This all looks wonderful, Elaine. You made gravy—how did you know it's one of my guilty pleasures? Thank you."

"I'm glad you said yes to dinner tonight or else I don't know what I would have done with it all." She felt a little sheepish as she poured their wine and then cut roast for both of them.

When they both were finally settled with food and drink, first bites taken and praised, Devon asked, "So you wanted to talk?"

Elaine looked down at her plate. Now or never.

"Devon, I owe you an apology."

"I suppose that depends on the reason you're apologizing."

"I know I sent mixed messages."

Devon took a sip of wine. "So why did you do it?"

Now comes the hard part. "Right before I took this assignment my ex moved out. It made our split final. I mean it was literally weeks that it took her to leave. But the truth is that the relationship had been over for a long time. We were more like roommates than lovers. I should have ended it a long time ago, but we were just so good at going through the motions."

"So why did it finally end?"

Elaine swallowed. "I can't tolerate cheaters and I made that clear from the beginning. But she cheated anyway. When I came up here it was to make peace with myself and everything that happened."

Devon digested this bit of information. "Are you still angry with her?" She reached across the table and took Elaine's hand.

Elaine certainly wasn't going to pull hers away even if Devon's caress was sending tiny shock waves up her arm that were making it difficult to concentrate.

"I don't think I'm as angry with what she did as how she did it. Everyone at our station knew. Well, everyone but my crew. They would have told me. But others bent over backward to keep Grace's secret. So I think my pride more than anything was hurt."

"Is Grace a good ranger?"

The question was insightful and totally unexpected. "Why do you ask?"

Devon shrugged. "Well, I imagine that part of the reason you are still at your station is because of your crew and their loyalty to you. But you don't strike me as the type of person who would stay after something like that occurred."

"I stay because it's home. My team is my family and I know that sooner or later the whispers will die out and there will be a new scandal to circulate. But to answer your question, Grace is not a good ranger. Shortly before I broke it off I found out that the only reason she has the job is because her daddy pulled some strings to get her a nice comfy desk job. She's expecting an inheritance and one condition of receiving that inheritance is that she works."

"And because your pride was publicly bruised it won't let you walk away?"

Elaine smiled. "Something like that."

Devon nodded. "Why didn't you tell me any of this before?"

"Because it wasn't until this last week when I was out doing patrols that I finally figured it out for myself."

"Okay."

"So will you forgive me?"

Devon was pensive for a moment. "On one condition."

"What's that?"

"Just try talking to me. Even if you don't know the words at least try. I would rather know that you don't know what to say than have you say nothing at all."

"I can do that."

Elaine was relieved to know that her actions hadn't caused a permanent rift between them. The conversation was once again relaxed and easy as they talked about what each had been doing during the week they spent apart.

Stomach full and glad of the electricity, Devon let Elaine talk her into catching up on work while Elaine did the dishes.

Dev,

Raine is doing quite well. We went to the doctor this morning and he said that an early delivery is possible. Your nephew shouldn't arrive for another few weeks yet, so please don't worry. I'll keep this short as I know how busy you must be. I hope the ranger isn't bothering you too much, he best keep his big, hairy paws off you. I know, I know, you can take care of yourself. I am very relieved to know that you aren't out in the snow freezing your ass off. Talk to you soon.

Take care. Love,

Stacey

Devon smiled as she read Stacey's e-mail. Stace hoped the ranger wasn't bothering her too much? How ironic that she'd chosen those words when Devon was very much bothered, hot and bothered!

As Devon closed her laptop and set it aside, she organized and gathered her notes before returning them to her bag. As she removed her glasses, the silence broke.

"Tell me about Stacey."

The question seemed to come out of nowhere. Devon looked at Elaine, who had been sitting across the room working quietly for the last little while, trying to figure out why she would ask. "What is it that you want to know?"

"You said she was your best friend. How did you two meet?"

Devon thought back and knew she was smiling. "I was thirteen and I had just moved into a new neighborhood. My dad got a job here in Washington State. It was hard leaving all my Oregon friends behind, but it was too good of an opportunity for him to pass up. I hadn't been out of the house much, but I finally worked up the courage to ride my bike around and see what my new surroundings had to offer. Stacey lived down the block. I damn near wrecked my bike when I saw her sunbathing."

"Sexy, huh?"

"Oh, yeah. Anyway, Stacey wasn't shy about anything. So we started hanging out. She was the first person I had ever met who made me realize that there were other people out there like me. Other girls who liked girls instead of boys." Devon laughed at the memory. "My parents loved her right away and began treating her like a daughter. We told each other everything. We still do. We became friends so fast and we spent so much time together that she felt more like a sister than a friend. We fought like sisters that's for sure. She even treated Raine like a sister. I was so young that it never even occurred to me that Stacey and I could be more than friends."

Elaine was busying herself with putting away cutlery. "Did you ever decide you could be?"

"We did talk about it once, what it would be like to take our friendship to a sexual level. So we kissed...once. There was nothing there. No sparks, no chemistry and we both agreed it was like kissing our sister. And that grossed us both out quite a bit."

Elaine laughed—did she sound relieved? Now that she understood Elaine's turmoil about her ex and her own future, Devon had to wonder exactly where she stood in Elaine's plans. A few kisses, or something more?

"Besides, our friendship was too important to risk. Stacey is the first person outside of my family that loved me unconditionally. And I love her the same way. But it never has been and never will be romantic love. Neither of us ever wants that to change."

"So did you two ever like the same women...ever compete?"

Devon hesitated for a moment before answering Elaine's question. It was better to get this out now. "No. Never. And neither of us will be in a relationship with someone who can't or won't accept our friendship."

"I'm sorry for asking. I didn't mean to pry. I was just curious."

Devon nodded in understanding.

"I can't believe anyone would be interested in *her* after meeting you." Elaine looked as if she hadn't meant to say the words out loud.

Devon was surprised by the remark and saw what she thought to be complete sincerity in Elaine's expression. Maybe she was just fishing when she asked softly, "What does that mean?"

Elaine smiled. "Don't get me wrong, your friend is attractive. I didn't mean to sound rude. It's just that...I mean, surely you know how beautiful and charming you are. I really can't imagine anyone not wanting to be with you."

Devon's breath caught, partly because of Elaine's words,

but more from the desire she saw simmering in Elaine's eyes. She felt herself flush and didn't know quite how to respond to the compliment. *Oh my God, I'm blushing?* Embarrassed, she focused on trying to hide her flushed cheeks, but she knew it was profoundly obvious.

"Thank you," she finally said. "That's nice of you to say. We need wood, right? I'll go."

Elaine watched Devon escape into the night, glad for once it wasn't her running for cover. She was surprised her honest compliment had perplexed Devon, who always seemed so poised.

Devon seemed more composed when she came back, leaving Elaine with her increasing struggle not to stare as Devon took care of the basic fire tending chores. She could stand in a corner all day and just watch the woman move.

Finished with the fire, Devon stretched and the T-shirt she was wearing lifted just enough for Elaine to see her midriff, firm and inviting. Elaine hoped that Devon hadn't heard her struggle for breath. Her body began to sweat and it had nothing to do with the now crackling fire. Those flames paled in comparison to the fire that Devon awakened in her.

It was going to be a very long night.

When Devon had kissed her, it seemed as though the world had spun around her. She just felt right. The feelings she had toward Devon were completely new to Elaine and she didn't know what to do with them.

It did no good to remind herself she was here to search for poachers and escape to the solitude of the mountains. She didn't need or want to feel this kind of desire for a woman who would be gone in a couple of weeks. Elaine wasn't ready for a fling and Devon definitely wasn't fling material.

Elaine couldn't presume that there would be a future for them off this mountain. How could she even entertain the possibility?

Devon raised her arms over her head, enjoying another good stretch before slipping away to the bathroom. Several minutes later she returned in shorts and another well-worn shirt. *My God, doesn't the woman own any clothes that aren't so sexy?*

Elaine quickly made her own escape to the bathroom. She had to leave the room or she couldn't be held responsible for her actions. She was finding it harder and harder to control her desire for Devon. The woman had her salivating like Pavlov's dog.

After she showered and brushed her teeth, Elaine finally returned to the main room, to find that Devon had already retired for the night. The only light still on was next to the chair. She glanced at the couch as she turned off the light and crawled into bed next to Devon. She knew she could sleep on the couch again, but couldn't resist sleeping next to Devon another night.

They lay still, not touching each other. Devon's back was to her and Elaine couldn't stand it. She wanted Devon to roll over. She wanted to look into her eyes. She wanted to feel that beautiful body pressed against hers. She wanted…

Elaine felt the long sleek body next to her tremble. "Are you cold?"

"No. I'm fine." The words were belied by a palpable shiver of the covers.

"Come here," Elaine gently commanded.

Elaine had only meant to hold Devon, to warm her, or at least that was what she told herself for the moments it took Devon to roll over. But as soon as Devon's body filled her arms, conscious thought escaped her and the desire that had been building all evening took over. With an uncontrollable hunger she claimed Devon's mouth. The voices that had been screaming all the reasons that she shouldn't be doing this were silenced as Devon's tongue slipped into her mouth. Her desire for Devon was all consuming and she was powerless against it.

Devon finally forced her arms to move long enough to push Elaine slightly away. "Elaine, please don't kiss me if you're going to stop there. I…I can't take it."

Elaine gazed down into the soft gray eyes that were illuminated by the fire and saw the vulnerability they reflected. She knew it was her own fault that Devon would be leery of her intentions. She lowered her head and placed another soft kiss on Devon's lips. She watched as Devon's eyes darkened with desire and she knew that she was beyond the point of return. How could she possibly not make love to Devon?

Elaine gently cupped Devon's cheek, her eyes intense as she quietly whispered, "I'm going to make love to you. I'm going to make love to you all night."

Elaine felt her soften, yielding in her arms. Devon moaned as Elaine bent her head to reclaim Devon's lips. She wrapped one arm around Devon, holding her close while the other hand cupped Devon's head, pulling her deeper into their kiss. Their kiss varied from deliciously gentle to probing and hungry. Elaine heard Devon whimper in surrender as she rolled her onto her back. "Elaine…"

"Yes, Devon…God, yes."

It was amazing how such simple words freed her mind, opened her body and sent any and all reservations fleeing. Suddenly, there were far too many clothes separating her body from Devon's, but she wasn't willing to stop kissing long enough to remove them. The breathless merging of their mouths and manic tasting of each other's lips and tongues continued until Elaine's need to feel Devon, all of her, became unbearable.

She nudged Devon's T-shirt upward, only to have Devon seize the hem and yank it off. Their impatience and growing need as they hastily removed the other's clothes only heightened Elaine's arousal.

"My God…you are so beautiful," Elaine whispered.

Devon placed a gentle hand on Elaine's cheek and slowly rubbed her thumb over Elaine's bottom lip. "Clearly you haven't looked in a mirror. You take my breath away."

"I haven't yet, but I certainly intend to," she murmured

against her lips before claiming them with a renewed hunger.

Bare, skin against skin, Elaine slowly lowered herself. Devon's legs naturally parted making room to cradle Elaine's hips. She gazed into Devon's eyes; eyes that reflected her trust and desire as she pulled Elaine's mouth to hers again.

Elaine was quickly consumed with Devon's long, deep, wet kisses that made her dizzy with need.

"Jesus, I love kissing you," Elaine whispered huskily. "You have been in my dreams every single night since the first day we met."

From the light of the burning fire and the moonlight filtering through the window, Elaine could see the fiery passion building in Devon's eyes. She moaned as Devon's hands slid down and stroked her breast. Elaine's nipples were firm and every part of her body responded to Devon's touch. She felt like she was going to melt from the heat of Devon's fingers.

Before Elaine could resist, Devon rolled her onto her back. Elaine opened her thighs to Devon's gentle insistence. Elaine's hips rocked against her and Devon's body molded to her, finding an answering rhythm. Every inch of skin that touched Devon's was on fire and it radiated down to the throbbing between her legs.

Devon kissed her neck, slowly and softly. Long, slow kisses trailed down across her chest to her breasts. Devon's mouth was greedy at Elaine's breast, opening to take more of her inside before swirling her tongue around Elaine's taut nipple.

With Devon's body moving against her own, Elaine sensed a woman who was starving to pleasure her as much as she longed to be pleasured. Devon's breath was heavy on her body and her eyes were bright with need. Her hands and mouth left no doubt that Devon wanted *her*. It was a feeling that Elaine had not experienced in a very long time.

When Devon's mouth moved to feast on her other breast she couldn't think. She could only feel…could only surrender to Devon's passion.

Devon's hands and mouth slowly explored her body, leaving a trail of wet kisses until Elaine's sweetness surrounded her. Devon was hungry to taste her. She had never before wanted a woman the way she wanted Elaine at that very moment. Elaine's body was so responsive to her touch and her hips rolled and pushed against her. She had never felt so primal. So aroused. So in control and out of control at the same time.

Elaine thought that she would lose her mind as Devon settled between her legs. Sure hands spread her thighs farther and Elaine closed her eyes in surrender.

At the first stroke of Devon's tongue, Elaine knew that it wouldn't take long for her to climax, something that had never been particularly easy for her.

"God, Elaine, you taste so good."

"Devon, you're driving me crazy."

Elaine was incredible and Devon wanted to savor every nuance, every taste, every moan. She could feel Elaine's body drawing closer to climax, but she wasn't ready for this to end. She had never enjoyed a woman so thoroughly. She felt intoxicated by Elaine and knew that once wouldn't be enough. Devon moved her mouth to Elaine's thigh, gently kissing and nipping.

"Please, Devon! Don't tease me...Please!"

Elaine's hands settled on the back of Devon's head guiding her mouth to where she so desperately needed it. Devon finally closed over her, letting her greedy tongue seek out Elaine's throbbing clit. She used her shoulders to push Elaine's legs up, spreading her, opening her completely. Elaine was unable to control her body as she felt the quiver in her thighs grow stronger.

Devon reached for Elaine's hands, using them to pull Elaine more firmly against her mouth. She delighted in Elaine writhing under her. She sucked Elaine hard into her mouth, her tongue playing over her.

"Oh, God! Don't stop!"

Elaine freed her hands, wrapping her fingers in Devon's hair, holding her mouth firmly against her aching body. Finally, with one hard thrust, Devon buried her tongue deep inside her. Elaine climaxed with a loud moan followed by a heavy gasp. Devon felt each quiver, each vibration emanate from Elaine's body.

Elaine finally released her hold on Devon's head, intending to pull her into her arms. She hadn't meant to hold Devon so hard against her. She wanted to be held by the woman who had so thoroughly ravaged her body. But Devon held her hips firmly and continued to stroke her gently with her tongue, dipping into her wetness, tasting her reward. This time the thundering in Elaine's ears didn't drown out the moans that she heard from Devon.

"Jesus, Devon!"

Elaine hadn't thought that her body would respond again so quickly. But Devon seemed to know just how she needed to be touched and licked, exactly what would make her body respond even after her climax just moments before.

"Fuck...Oh my God!" Elaine screamed as the feeling intensified once more.

Devon's hands smoothed over her belly, down across her hips and thighs. She intended to go slow this time, to take her time, but she just couldn't control herself as she pulled Elaine's hips more firmly to her mouth. When her tongue had first dipped into Elaine, a craving had careened through her body and she knew it wouldn't soon be satisfied. She reveled in Elaine's moans of pleasure driving her to continue.

Elaine climaxed again with more force than she could have imagined. Devon never lost her rhythm, never quit stroking her. Elaine heard herself begging, but hardly recognized the voice as her own. She couldn't see beyond the bright flashes of light behind her eyelids as her back arched urging Devon to bury her face deeper. And Devon did, greedily taking everything that

Elaine had to offer.

Devon finally lay with her head resting on Elaine's thigh, feeling it quiver under her cheek as she softly caressed Elaine's stomach, allowing her to catch her breath. Just as Elaine was about to ask Devon to come and hold her, she felt Devon's fingers slide inside her body.

Elaine had rarely been able to orgasm twice and never so close together. In truth, she had always been grateful to achieve orgasm once. But twice was an anomaly and three times…well, that just didn't happen to Elaine. But Devon wasn't done with her. She wanted to tell Devon that she couldn't again. She didn't want to disappoint Devon by not reaching another orgasm, but before she could even complete her thoughts, she felt her body responding yet again. Devon slid in and out of Elaine, at first slow and gentle, as she enjoyed the feel of Elaine's warm center as the silky wetness enveloped her fingers. The unhurried and tender pace made way for a faster, deeper motion that left Elaine wondering how she could have ever doubted Devon and her ability to bring her to climax *again*.

"Jesus, Devon, fuck me," she pleaded.

Devon continued her quest, her single-minded pursuit to give Elaine pleasure. She curled her fingers deep inside Elaine's body and felt the tight muscles tug at her fingers. Devon held her eyes on Elaine, watching her beautiful face display her pleasure. As Elaine's body began to tighten, Devon finally lowered her mouth to Elaine once more pushing her to heights she had never imagined or experienced before.

Devon's tongue perfectly matched the rhythm of her fingers.

Elaine was beyond thought, beyond herself. She felt her body gathering and tightening, as Devon's name once again rolled off her lips. Never before had she screamed out her pleasure, but with Devon she had no control.

She gasped for breath as her body pulsed and tightened around Devon's fingers. Devon willingly gave everything that Elaine asked for and more. Devon didn't stop until the last moan;

the last vestiges of orgasm were wrung from Elaine's body. She raised Elaine's hips higher allowing her full access to drink in every last drop of Elaine's pleasure. God, had any woman ever tasted so good? Had any woman ever been so wet, so ready for her? No, never before.

Elaine felt completely exhausted; replete with satisfaction. How had Devon known what her body wanted and needed when she hadn't even known herself? Dr. Devon McKinney was an entirely new experience for Elaine.

Devon finally crawled up next to Elaine and pulled her spent body into her arms, gently cradling her. She hadn't wanted to stop. The taste, the intricately changing textures, the way Elaine had moved against her, offering herself so completely had been thrilling. She had been greedy for more. She knew that she could easily stay buried between Elaine's thighs all night.

With her past lovers, not that there had been many since her focus on work had been such a hindrance to meeting people, Devon had been more reserved, almost shy. She hadn't been so aggressive and she feared that Elaine might not like it. But when she heard Elaine's moans and her ragged pleading, she had been unable to stop herself. The silken folds and sweet taste wouldn't allow her to stop. Never had she reveled in a woman's desire the way she had Elaine's. Devon instinctively knew that she would never crave another woman this way.

Elaine listened to Devon's strong, steady heartbeat beneath her ear. She wasn't accustomed to being treated this way; she had always been the one to satisfy her lover's needs. She had always been in control, the one that was needed to satisfy someone else. She had never been in this position before.

"Are you okay?"

She sighed and moved closer to Devon. "Much better than okay. That was amazing. *You* are amazing."

Devon's arms tightened around her. For the first time in her life she understood what it felt like to have someone put her needs first. She had trusted Devon completely, instinctively knowing that Devon would take care of her and she *felt* safe.

Devon's hands wandered aimlessly over Elaine's back as if she couldn't stop caressing the skin beneath her fingers.

After several minutes, Elaine stirred, her breathing steadied and she found her voice.

"Thank you for that."

Devon's smile was gentle as she brushed a stray lock of hair out of Elaine's eyes.

"Believe me, the pleasure was all mine."

Elaine leaned into Devon, intending the kiss to be gentle. But when she tasted herself on Devon's lips, the all-consuming fire returned. It was her turn to feed her hunger—her turn to savor Devon and quench her own thirst. Her turn to pleasure Devon as thoroughly as Devon had pleasured her. She slid on top of Devon using one hand to hold Devon's arms above her head as she kissed her. With her free hand she began to explore Devon's body and the low, sultry moans she heard thrilled her, sending sensations up and down her spine.

She took her time getting acquainted with Devon's body, kissing Devon's neck before moving slowly to her breast. Playfully nipping and licking the little crease just at her shoulder, she tasted the mint flavor that permeated all of Devon's skin. The softness just under the swell of her breasts was slightly warmer and Elaine took her time with the subtle changes of Devon's beautiful body. Her hand slowly continued to wander as Devon urged her back for another deep kiss.

"Jesus, Elaine..."

Elaine smiled against her skin as she pressed her hips against Devon. She felt Devon immediately raise her body seeking more.

Elaine slowly slid her hand between their bodies. She kissed Devon gently as her fingers glided smoothly between sensitive folds. "You're so wet. God, I love that."

Devon's eyes slid shut and Elaine stilled her hand.

"Look at me." She waited patiently as Devon raised her head, folding the pillow beneath her head in half to prop herself up and their eyes met.

"I want to watch you."

She held Devon's gaze as her fingers began to move again. Her heart skipped a beat the moment she saw her own feelings of trust and surrender mirrored in Devon's eyes. She eased gently between Devon's parted legs, enjoying the feel of Devon's hips molding against her own. She bent to take a hard nipple between her teeth as her fingers continued their discovery.

Elaine's fingers played over the wet delicate tissue, learning how Devon liked to be touched. Without a single word, Elaine knew exactly what would please her. She had never been so sure of what a lover wanted; her every touch, every stroke, elicited moans of pleasure. She plunged her fingers deeper.

Devon gasped, her body arching to meet each hard thrust as Elaine used her hips to drive even deeper. She teased Devon's clit with her thumb, feeling it throb beneath the gentle pressure.

Devon buried her face in Elaine's neck, whispering her name again and again, each thrust bringing her closer. Finally her body stiffened and her breath caught as wave after wave of orgasm crashed through her body.

Elaine held her gently as she tried to catch her breath. The low light from the fire played across Devon's skin. Elaine's eyes traveled down Devon's body. She wanted to taste Devon... *needed* to taste her.

Devon's breathing hadn't quite returned to normal when Elaine began kissing her way down her body. Elaine used her knees to gently urge Devon's legs apart. It only took a few minutes before Devon's body was rocking against Elaine's tongue in climax.

The fire snapped and crackled and the wind blew, but the only thing that Elaine could hear was her name being torn from Devon's lips. It was the most exquisite sound she had ever heard.

They lay wrapped in each other's arms, murmuring their complete satisfaction. Devon rested her head on Elaine's shoulder with their arms and legs entwined as sleep claimed them both.

Devon stirred during the night looking for blankets. The fire had died down and the temperature in the room had dropped. She reached for the blanket that had slid down the length of their bodies. Elaine reached out and found Devon's chilled body, pulling it against her own to warm her. Devon felt every nerve in her body ignite as she rolled over to see Elaine's eyes lock on her own. Elaine sleepily pressed her soft lips to Devon's forehead as they quickly fell back to sleep. Wrapped comfortably in each other arms, they awoke throughout the night to make love again.

Chapter 11

The morning light filtered in the large cabin windows as they lay wrapped in each other's arms. Elaine had never wanted a woman the way she wanted Devon. She had been insatiable. She remembered the first night that she and Grace had slept together; it hadn't been anything like her night with Devon. At the time she had thought that it was good, but she didn't have the overwhelming need to constantly touch and kiss her like she had with Devon. The sensual touches that communicated what words couldn't exposed the truth about the charade her relationship with Grace had been. Sex with her had been tactical, even manipulative. Grace had never wanted her, had never *needed* her the way Devon had.

"Good morning." Elaine smiled, her voice husky.

God, she has a sexy voice. Devon rested her chin on the arm that she had crossed over Elaine's chest, then arched up to meet Elaine's lips for a long, lingering kiss. "Good morning, yourself."

She suddenly felt shy and somewhat vulnerable. She knew it was silly. They had shared a night of intense passion and Elaine had acquainted herself with every inch of Devon's body. But today she had to return to her work and she wondered if she would see Elaine again or if one night was all they would have. Maybe it was all that Elaine even wanted.

Her thoughts were interrupted by the static and garbled voice emanating from the radio. Elaine sighed and reluctantly extricated herself from Devon. Elaine slipped on her slippers before padding across the cold floor.

Devon propped herself up on her elbows enjoying the view as she watched Elaine's nude body cross the room. She listened as Elaine confirmed her position and then a series of numbers and coordinates were given by the messenger. Elaine quickly scribbled down the information and told the person on the other end that she was on her way.

"There's a problem on the south rim. I've got to go." She pulled on clothes at a rapid pace. "Lost hiker."

"It's okay. I understand. Duty calls."

"This is definitely not how I wanted this morning to go." She leaned in for a kiss and it was several minutes before she finally pulled away.

"Be careful," Devon said.

"God, I wish I didn't have to go." Elaine whispered before turning to pick up her pack and rifle. Without another word she was out the door.

When Devon heard the truck start and leave, she rolled onto her back, put an arm over her eyes and sighed. Last night was a wonderful foray, but she still had work to do. After a moment, she crawled from the bed and headed for the shower.

She dressed and made the bed as memories of the night before flashed through her mind. Elaine was an amazing woman and an extraordinary lover. She had never thought she would meet a woman like Elaine, much less find her on the side of a damn mountain.

From inside her tent she retrieved a small shovel, brush and clipboard. She stood for a moment watching as her breath formed clouds in the air. The temperature would help keep her awake after the few hours of sleep she had managed. Staying awake and staying focused were two different things entirely.

The sun was slipping behind the mountain by the time she realized what time it was. She had just enough light to gather some wood from the pile she had made and get a fire going before the sun was completely gone. With a lantern, she sat on a log near the fire wrapped in a blanket. She couldn't tell if she was numb from the hours of working in the cold or pure physical exhaustion.

As she watched the flames dance in the breeze, she was reminded of the way the fire played over Elaine's bronze skin. Of how the fire reflected in her eyes and how it had seemed that Elaine could see directly into her heart. The flames continued their sensuous movements and she could almost feel the way Elaine's body had moved against her.

She banked the fire, made certain the grate was securely over it and took her battery operated lantern into her tent.

She checked her watch again and sighed. This would be a good time to call Stacey. She had always looked forward to these phone calls, but tonight she just wanted to be alone with her thoughts. As she dialed the number she hoped the static would conceal how she was feeling.

"Hey Stace, it's me." The static was indeed terrible.

"Dev? What's wrong?"

She should have known better. At least she could give Stacey part of the truth. She certainly wasn't going to tell her about the night she spent in Elaine's arms right now.

"I'm tired and cold. I was just calling to check in and see how you and Raine are doing."

"Raine is fine. She says I'm driving her crazy."

Devon laughed. "I'm sure she does. Any change?"

"No. The doctor says that we still have at least a couple of weeks."

"How are you?"

"I'm fine. But there is something you aren't telling me."

She smiled. Stacey could always read her so well. "The static is terrible and I'm just really tired."

Even through the static she could hear Stacey sigh. "Who is she?"

She laughed outright. "I'm about a thousand miles from civilization, why would you assume there is a woman involved?"

"Because I know you, sweetie. And I know women and that tone always means there is a woman involved. Spill it."

"You're impossible, you know that, right?" She tried to deflect her. "We're talking about me not you."

Stacey laughed softly. "Okay, so you slept with her. What's the problem?"

"You really aren't going to let this go are you?" God she wished she could have this conversation without so much damn static.

"I will once you tell me what's really going on."

She really should have known that Stacey would discern she was leaving something out. She may as well save herself the trouble and just tell her.

"Okay fine. I'm tired because I just spent last night having incredible sex with the ranger who is assigned to watch over me."

"And?"

"And nothing. I'm attracted to her."

"I would certainly hope so. I would worry if you had sex with a woman you weren't attracted to." Stacey's timely sarcasm made her smile.

"Stacey, I'm…I'm *insanely* attracted to her. When it snowed and we were in the cabin, we spent hours talking. I felt so comfortable with her."

The static was almost deafening while she waited for Stacey to respond.

"Devon, are you falling in love with her?"

She tried to ignore her heart hammering in her chest. "It's a little too soon for that, don't you think?"

She could hear the playfulness in Stacey's words. "I don't think I'm the person to answer that. Do you?"

She laughed. "No. I suppose not."

"Does this ranger have a name?"

"Elaine." *Damn, just saying her name makes me quiver.*

"So where is ranger Elaine now?"

"She was called out to work early this morning and I came back to my camp to work."

"And you don't know how she feels about you, but you want to?"

"Well, yeah, something like that. What the hell is my problem?"

"Devon, love, you and I both know that you aren't like me. You can't just have sex with a woman and move on. It's much deeper for you and I doubt you would have slept with her if you didn't feel something other than pure sexual desire."

She knew that Stacey's comment was really an open-ended question. "There is just something about her."

"Good sex?"

"Mind-blowing." She could hear the exhilaration in her own voice. "I have *never* been so aggressive, insatiable, or satisfied."

Stacey laughed. "I knew there was hope for you!"

"You can be such a guy sometimes!"

"No love, I'm a woman that loves sex with other women. There's a *huge* difference."

Yes, Stacey was definitely a woman who loved sex, God love her. "I just don't know what I should do."

"It's obvious you want to see her again, yes?"

"Of course."

"And she said nothing about wanting to see you again?"

"No, but there was almost no time for it. Still..."

"Did you tell her what you wanted?"

Devon slowly answered, "No, she had to go."

"Unless your ranger is a psychic, it seems to me that you have two choices."

Devon already knew the answer but asked anyway. "Which are?"

"You can either accept the fact that you had one night of great sex and leave it at that, or you can track her down and tell her that you want more."

"Gee, you think? Thanks for stating the obvious, oh wise one."

"My little Dev is growing up. She finally realizes I'm wise." Stacey's twisted sense of humor made her laugh. "Seriously, I know that you don't do one night-stands. But you won't know if that's all it was unless you tell her how you feel, or she tells you. You just need to do what makes you happy."

"Thanks, Stace." She winced as static crackled again.

"Let me know what you decide?"

"I will. Have a good night."

"You too. Sleep well. I love you."

"I love you too. Sweet dreams."

Devon hung up her phone, glad to have the static in her ear silenced. She sank back into her bed pondering Stacey's advice. The first choice didn't seem much like a choice at all. Letting it go, without knowing, that just didn't seem possible.

Elaine had been called away for work. There really had been no time for them to discuss if their night together would be all that there was. Her gut told her that wasn't the case. After all, Elaine had come to her campsite to seek her out, invite her to dinner and talk about what had already happened between them...before they ever had sex. Everything inside her told her it wasn't just a one-night stand, not for her or Elaine.

She was a scientist first and foremost and as a scientist she knew better than to let herself get ahead of the evidence. Of course, when there was an opportunity, she would gather more facts from Elaine. The simple truth was that she had shared a wonderful night of sex with an amazing woman, but it was equally indisputable that she still had work to complete.

Her time in the cabin with Elaine the week before, or their amazing night of passion together didn't change that. She had worked quickly and efficiently on this assignment and as a result only expected to be on location another week or so. If she saw Elaine again, that would be great. If not, maybe she would look her up when she got back home. No sense dwelling on unanswered questions. She knew she already had plenty on her plate, including a research deadline and a pregnant sister to get back to.

Chapter 12

Morning hadn't come soon enough for Elaine as she made her way down the mountain. The hike seemed to take forever and the closer she got to Devon's camp, the more questions began plaguing her mind. *Would Devon even want to see her? Would she welcome Elaine's presence or see it as an intrusion upon her and her work?*

After receiving the early morning call the day before, she had been forced to leave the cabin and Devon, far sooner than she would have liked. When she had arrived at her destination and had been informed that the lost hiker had found his group, she was relieved. Not only for the hiker's safety, but because it meant that she could quickly return to the cabin and to Devon.

When she had returned and found Devon gone she hadn't really been surprised. She knew Devon had a job to do and was committed to it. She didn't expect their incredible night together to interfere with Devon's responsibilities. Elaine was also fully aware that Devon was anxious to get home to her sister and help prepare for the birth of her nephew. The sooner she finished her assignment, the sooner she could do that.

Elaine had spent their day apart reliving the night before as she searched the area for signs of poachers. She tried not to hope that Devon would be at the cabin when she returned for the night. She was still disappointed to find that Devon had chosen so stay at her camp, but the fact was that Devon had no way of knowing how long Elaine would be gone and Elaine didn't really believe that Devon was the kind of woman who would show up unannounced or uninvited on the off chance that Elaine made it back that night.

If it hadn't been so dark and it hadn't taken her so long to do a sweep of the area, perhaps she would have made her way down the mountain to seek out Devon. Dr. McKinney certainly had a way about her. She had brought out a side of herself that she had never known existed. It was freeing she realized, in as much as it was frightening.

But instead of going down the mountain in the pitch dark, bitter cold night air, she stayed in the cabin and attempted to get some rest. But sleep hadn't come easy. She craved the feel of Devon's body next to hers. She could still smell Devon on the pillow and she wanted her there more than anything.

As she tossed and turned, she tried to find some kind of balance.

She would persuade herself to give Devon time and space to work, while she used the time to think, maybe sort out her feelings about the intimate encounter with the other woman. She knew she needed to think about what was happening, what had happened. There were many reasons they shouldn't have slept together. *Slept? They had certainly done little of that.* Then she'd think about the magic of the night and wonder if it really was all that dark and dangerous for a midnight hike.

Elaine didn't have a multitude of past sexual experiences to compare Devon to, but she didn't need them to know that she would never again meet another woman like her. Devon hadn't tried to hide her desire or pleasure when she touched Elaine and she had been wonderfully responsive. The pleasure that Devon drew from everything they had shared was clear and Elaine loved that about her.

Her entire experience with Devon had been completely different than anything she had ever shared with Grace. Thanks to Devon, she now knew what it was like to be with someone who took equal pleasure in giving and receiving. Devon and Grace were like night and day. Both in and out of bed.

As dawn approached she had confronted the real source of her fears and uncertainties: her attraction to Devon was no longer just physical. After the long day apart, she knew she wanted to pursue more with Devon. She didn't want just a casual affair. She only hoped that Devon wanted the same thing.

As Elaine approached Devon's camp, she understood at least one reason why Devon may have chosen the stay at her campsite the night before. The hike down the mountain had been treacherous. Patches of ice covered the rocks, making it difficult to maintain her footing. Thankfully, there was just enough snow to give her *some* traction and plenty of branches for her to cling to when she felt herself sliding. Upon reaching Devon's camp, she spotted her hard at work and couldn't help but stand and admire the vision before her.

Devon had obviously not heard her coming as she knelt over a cleared patch of soil, seeming completely focused on her work. When Devon finally stood to stretch, Elaine hadn't even realized that she had moved until her arms were wrapped effortlessly around Devon's waist and the words, "Good morning," had crossed her lips.

The questions and fears that had flooded Elaine's mind on the hike down were squashed when she felt Devon turn in her arms and pull her closer for a slow kiss. Devon's sultry moans and parted lips invited Elaine to deepen the kiss. She pulled Devon tighter into her arms and felt the shiver that traveled the length of Devon's body. Elaine's hands ached to touch her bare skin. For the briefest of moments she thought of inviting Devon back to the cabin, but she was far too aroused for that. Her desire was blazing and her need to feel Devon would wait no longer.

"I know you still have work to do and I promise I will help you catch up. But right now I really want you…need you." Her voice broke. This was so unlike her, but all her thoughts and plans seemed pointless now that she had Devon near again.

The trees were spinning all around her and the only thing Devon could focus on was Elaine and her dark, hypnotic gaze. It pleaded with her, but all she could hear was the pounding of her own heart. She was deeply pleased that Elaine had come for her and Stacey's know-it-all advice was moot. Though she hadn't heard Elaine's words, she answered the question in Elaine's eyes with, "Yes."

Elaine took Devon's hand and led her to the tent. The truth was that the hard, snow-covered ground would do just fine, but the tent's snug confines were perfect. She was hardly worried about them getting cold, the heat radiating from their desire alone was enough and she was sure that there were plenty of pleasant ways to continue keeping each other warm.

Once they were inside, they quickly stripped off the offending clothes in a frenzy of burning kisses. Devon lay completely naked; her arms open and reaching, welcoming Elaine in for a long languid kiss. "I need you."

The words sent a quiver of longing through Elaine's entire body. The lust burning in Devon's eyes rivaled her own. She had never before known what it felt like to be needed or wanted so badly.

"Anything you want, Devon, anything at all."

Devon brought Elaine's hand urgently to her body where Elaine's nimble fingers began stroking her already ample wetness, answering Devon's plea. Devon's words were interrupted by short raspy gasps making the actual words impossible to understand, but Elaine knew what they meant.

Devon's hand rested upon her own, guiding her as she gently stroked her, filling Elaine with the knowledge that she was doing exactly what Devon wanted. Faster and firmer when Devon needed it and then more slowly, just enough to tease her and heighten her arousal. Devon's body moved faster against Elaine's hand and became more rigid as she pleaded, "I need to feel you inside me. Please."

Elaine felt her own clit throb in response as Devon's body yielded to her.

"More, please, more," Devon begged as Elaine slid another finger into Devon. "Oh God, that feels so good. Faster. Oh God, please."

Elaine, wanting nothing more than to please the beautiful woman in her arms, did exactly as she was asked. When she felt Devon's body begin to tighten and arch, she pulled her fingers out to stroke Devon's rigid clit. Devon climaxed with a low groan that started deep within her body and was finally ripped from her in exhausting pleasure.

She lay panting in Elaine's arms, struggling for breath. In spite of Devon's obvious fatigue, Elaine couldn't pry her hands from Devon's body, instead she continued the slow steady stroking of Devon's clit. Elaine whispered, "I'm sorry, Devon."

Devon couldn't help but hold her breath until Elaine explained.

"I'm sorry for the way I left the other morning." Elaine smiled, "And I'm profusely thankful that you have such a comfortable sleeping arrangement."

Struggling to find her voice with such distracting things happening between her legs, Devon managed to say, "I'm glad you approve."

"Definitely," Elaine replied as she began to playfully nibble and kiss Devon's lips.

The playful moment turned intense as Elaine's touch became more deliberate, letting the deep rolling of Devon's hips guide her. Elaine held Devon's gaze, watching the gray pools darken until they appeared almost black.

"Will you come for me?" Elaine whispered as she plunged her fingers forcefully inside Devon. Sliding between Devon's parted thighs, Elaine found Devon's tempo.

"Oh…My…God. Yes, just like that."

"I asked you a question." Elaine marveled at the degree of Devon's surrender.

Devon sounded as though she might cry when she finally moaned, "Yes. Just don't stop. Please don't stop."

"I'm not stopping. You know I won't stop. Come for me."

"Harder!"

Elaine watched the pleasure play across Devon's face. She felt powerful. She felt completely desired and needed. Devon's body and its every movement communicated to Elaine exactly what she liked and Elaine committed it all to memory.

Devon pulled Elaine down for a ravenous kiss as her hips bucked and arched into climax. When Devon tightened around her fingers, Elaine matched it with a moan of her own. *Everything about this woman is phenomenal.*

Elaine lay holding Devon as her breathing slowed. She could feel the warmth of her breath on her shoulder and for a brief moment thought to herself that she would like nothing more than to be in this position with Devon for the rest of her life. She was willing to leave the moment perfect unto itself. She could ignore the throbbing between her legs. She had gotten what her body had been crying out for…Devon.

Devon lay exhausted and content, curled up tight against Elaine as she nuzzled deeper into her shoulder. She never knew she could feel so sexually confident and comfortable with another woman, but with Elaine she was both. She was a fabulous lover, but there was more...more that made Devon feel like it was safe to open herself up to her, physically and emotionally.

Devon quietly whispered, "Thank you. And I'm sorry for being so demanding. I feel like I just can't get enough of you."

"I think I'm the one who should be thanking you and *never* apologize for that."

Devon was quiet, her words barely audible. "I wasn't sure I would see you again."

Elaine placed a finger under Devon's chin tilting her head up until gray eyes met obsidian. With a gentle smile she said, "I wasn't sure you would want to see me." With a slight shrug she added, "But I couldn't stay away."

Devon felt the tears well up and she tried to push them down. She cupped Elaine's cheek, "I'm so very glad that you couldn't."

Elaine's eyes reflected more than a physical need. A thousand butterflies took flight in her stomach as she interpreted Elaine's expression. Devon knew at that moment that this was more than just sex for both of them. The thousand butterflies turned into a thousand questions...for later. Right now, there was just the two of them.

Elaine whispered, "I didn't want to leave yesterday morning, but I knew that if I didn't go quickly, then I wouldn't have left at all." She gently tasted Devon's lips. "I missed you last night."

Devon was as helpless to control the pounding of her heart as she was to stop her hands wandering over Elaine's body, mapping every curve, every plane. "I missed you too and I'm *very* happy you're here now." Devon was quiet for a moment before meeting Elaine's eyes. "Elaine, I understand you have a job to do. We both do. And our jobs mean a lot to each of us. So please don't ever apologize for having to work. The only reason I wasn't sure if I would see you again is because we hadn't talked about it. We didn't have the chance to before you were called out. So I was unsure if that was all you wanted."

Elaine's gaze never wavered as she looked into Devon's eyes. For a moment she looked petrified, then her expression steadied. "I want more than just one night or two nights with you."

The admission took Devon's breath away. She had to swallow hard before she could say, "I want more than one or two nights with you as well."

Elaine's heart hammered against Devon's ear, then quieted. Devon was content to let them both calm down.

After a minute, Elaine chuckled and said, "I'm glad to hear that. I took a chance coming to your camp today, you know. I figured that if you didn't want to see me, the worst that could happen is that I would find myself hanging upside down in a tree. Being the accomplished woodsman you are, I thought you might have set a trap for an unwanted intruder."

The laughter settled Devon's nerves. How wonderful was this, cuddled in her lover's arms, sharing such a pleasant afterglow?

Laughter fading, Elaine rolled Devon onto her back. "I think you should show me just how happy you are that I'm here and how much you missed me."

Her voice sounding sultry to her own ears, Devon said, "I hear a command in there, Captain."

She rolled Elaine onto her back in one quick motion finding Elaine's lips. This wasn't what Elaine had intended but her body grew heavy with arousal at Devon's aggressiveness.

The fire rapidly grew into a blaze as their breath merged. Devon's lips slowly traced a path from her jaw to her ear and ever so slowly down her neck before moving lower to capture a firm nipple between her teeth. Elaine's wordless ecstasy fueled the flames burning out of control in Devon. Her need pushed her lower, as she settled between Elaine's trembling thighs.

"You're such a tease. You're killing me. Please?"

"Don't worry, Captain, I'll give you everything you want and need." With a deep feral growl, Devon buried her face between Elaine's thighs as she sank two fingers deep within her. The thrusting of her fingers was the perfect complement to the delightful motions of her tongue. Elaine's hips instinctively rose as she silently begged for more.

Devon paused as she tilted her head and ran her finger along Elaine's smooth stomach. "Don't you know that all I want to do is pleasure you?"

Elaine knew better than to try and speak. She could only hope that her eyes were telling Devon everything she felt.

Devon's smile was that of a confident seductress. Again Elaine watched Devon's mouth lower to her body. She gently kissed Elaine's inner thigh, then moved her mouth slowly over her. She could only imagine the gift awaiting her.

With a firm hand, Devon brought Elaine fiercely against her mouth. She had fantasized about this, spent hours the night before remembering how Elaine had tasted. She wasn't willing to fantasize any longer, finally she had Elaine right where she wanted her...pressed firmly against her tongue. As she slid her tongue up and down, between the folds of Elaine's body, she was intoxicated by everything that was uniquely Elaine. Suddenly she felt Elaine's strong thighs wrap around her. Devon didn't think there could be anything more erotic than having Elaine hold her firmly in place, directing her to the precise place she wanted her mouth. Long strides of her tongue made way for the lighter flicking over Elaine's engorged clit. The fire she had wanted to build in Elaine was already ablaze. With a steady rhythm, Elaine raised and lowered her hips as she ground herself hard against Devon's face. Elaine raised her hips higher, letting out a deep gasp followed by a long moan. Devon matched her as her mouth was flooded with Elaine's desire. She drank thirstily before slowly dragging her tongue up to bring Elaine's clit fully into her mouth. Elaine's hips moved wildly against Devon before rising one final time. With a primal scream, Elaine climaxed.

As they lay holding one another, a loud growl emanated from Devon's stomach.

Elaine kissed her forehead tenderly and laughed. "I think we should take care of that."

"You know my food supply is limited. I don't have much in the way of variety."

"I'm a ranger. I'm prepared for any situation and I think you might like what I have in mind." They left the tent and Devon collected some firewood from the pile she kept under a small tarp to keep it dry.

"You're quite the girl scout aren't you?"

Devon laughed. "Hardly! I've just learned from experience."

Elaine retrieved the backpack that she had left next to a tree. From it she produced two foil-wrapped packages.

"I hope you don't mind my campfire special."

Devon finished placing the grate over the fire. "Right now I could eat tree bark. Anything is better than more freeze-dried stuff."

Elaine smiled. "Hopefully you'll find this a little more appetizing."

"What is it we are having for lunch?"

"It's a surprise."

She edged the packets close to the fire where there would be sufficient heat for them to cook, but could still be easily retrieved.

"This is an interesting contraption." Elaine indicated the grate over the fire.

"I had it fabricated at a metal shop. The holes are small enough to keep the embers in while letting the smoke and heat out. They made it so it's foldable to fit in my pack."

Elaine looked at the grate again and was amazed at the ingenuity of the design. "Is there anything you haven't thought of?"

Devon walked over and dropped a lingering kiss on Elaine's lips. "Probably, but I've learned a lot from trial and error."

While the meal was cooking, Devon found a blanket. Elaine

sat on a small foam pad with her back against a log. Devon slid between Elaine's legs leaning back against her chest enjoying the strong arms that circled around her, holding her close. The snow that surrounded them made the air cold, but Elaine did a fine job of keeping Devon warm. At that moment Devon wouldn't have cared if it was fifty below zero.

The aroma of food filled the air and the fire reflected just out of the corner of Devon's eye. She turned and for the first time and noticed the rifle lying just a few feet from Elaine. Elaine observed the expression on Devon's face as she looked at the rifle. Remembering the circumstances surrounding the death of Devon's parents, Elaine asked, "Does it bother you?"

Devon turned to kiss her. "I thought it would, but it doesn't."

"You should carry one, you know."

"I've been told that and I actually do have a gun, believe it or not. It is secured in my home safe."

"I understand, but it doesn't do you a lot of good there, when you are out here." Elaine's concern was evident. "What if an animal came after you?"

"Then a gun probably wouldn't do me much good anyway. I doubt I would even hit the predator. No matter how much I practice, I can't hit the broad side of a barn."

Elaine laughed. Devon's honesty was refreshing. She suppressed the alarming feeling that suddenly overcame her. She didn't want anything happening to Devon. She had obviously survived on her own, but still, Devon shouldn't take chances.

They continued to sit wrapped in each other's arms until Devon's stomach growled again. She pulled away slightly, "I think you said something about feeding me?"

Elaine couldn't help but laugh. "Yes, ma'am, I believe I did."

She pulled the foil-wrapped packages out of the fire while Devon found plates and forks. Elaine carefully placed the grate back over the fire making certain that it was indeed doing its job.

Devon deeply inhaled the aroma of steak and vegetables. "I never fathomed that I would be eating steak on this assignment.

A pleasant surprise, I must say." She handed Elaine a bottle of water and settled next to her on the log pulling the blanket over their laps.

"God, this is delicious."

"I'm sure it is, compared to tree bark."

Devon bumped her playfully with her shoulder, but said nothing as she ate. Elaine was pleased to see that Devon was enjoying her meal. *I want to have dinner with her every night for the rest of my life.* That thought had come out of nowhere and took Elaine completely by surprise. They finished eating quickly and tidied up.

Stomach satisfied, but not yet able to suggest a return to work, Devon settled back into Elaine's arms, leaning her head back against Elaine's shoulder. Devon could easily imagine doing this every night. *So why does the thought scare me so damn much?*

To prevent herself from dwelling on the unsettling question she said, "I thought most ranger cabins were located near an observation tower."

"They are and we do have a tower at the top of this ridge." Elaine said, pointing up. "But several years ago a fire came through here and burned down the old cabin. When we were trying to get to the blaze we created the road that leads up there now. It just seemed like the right place to rebuild. We designed this cabin with a glass front and deck so that a ranger could still see what was going on in the canyon below. It's nice to have a cabin designed so that we can lock a generator nearby, keep a dry stack of wood and a collection tank for water. No one wants to be in the cabin with a fire sneaking over the ridge behind them."

Devon shivered at the thought. "Do you work the tower?"

Elaine pulled her close trying to quell the shiver. "Satellites do most of that now. I have more training duties than anything else, but I get out in the field as often as I can. Since I made captain, I have a lot more paperwork to contend with."

Devon turned to look at Elaine. "Is it standard protocol for you to be out here by yourself?"

"Not usually, but there isn't much activity up here this time of year. Like I mentioned before, we have had some reports of poaching, but I haven't seen any signs of it yet. Besides," Elaine added with a lazy smile and wink, "not much paperwork followed me up here and I have a botanist to watch over."

Devon poked Elaine in the ribs making her laugh again, before silencing her with a long deep kiss.

Chapter 13

Devon hated how slow her laptop was with the wireless card, even from the top of the ridge, happily ensconced on Elaine's couch. Oh well, at least she was still able to access the Internet. She hurried through her work e-mails and let her supervisor know that she was ahead of schedule. She sent in her daily reports and analysis and then turned to her sister's e-mail.

Hey Sis,

I'm sure Stacey is keeping you updated. I spoke with Phillip today. He said it put his mind at ease that Stacey is so attentive. She is driving me crazy, can't you talk to her? Your nephew is kicking the hell out of me. I think he may become a soccer player! The doctor keeps saying it will be a couple of weeks. Didn't he say that a couple of weeks ago? I can't wait to get his foot out of my ribs! I miss you. Be safe. Come home soon.

I love you,
Raine

Devon smiled as she read her sister's message. She wished she could be there to feel her nephew kick. She looked across the room at Elaine and was once again torn between her desire to be with her sister and to stay right where she was.

Elaine caught her looking. "Is everything okay?"

Devon smiled reassuringly. "Yes. I just read an e-mail from Raine. She told me about my nephew kicking." Her smile grew distant and wistful, almost sad. "I miss my sister."

Elaine's voice was a bit tighter as she said, "You'll be able to go home and see her soon."

After a moment she tore her gaze from Elaine's redirecting it to her e-mail. She noticed another e-mail from Stacey, but before opening it she typed a quick reply to Raine. She wanted to reassure her that she would be back for the birth of the baby and tell her how much she missed her. Nothing would keep her from being there for her sister and her nephew, even if she was conflicted.

Devon patiently waited for Stacey's message to open, once again slightly frustrated at the poor connection she had while in the field.

Hey Love,

Took Raine to the doctor again today. The most recent due date seems to be correct. He said that while she still has some time, there is little doubt that she will go into labor sooner than he originally thought. Everything is good here. Your plants look beautiful. We definitely need to talk when you get back. I have something that I need to discuss with you. How are things with the Ranger?

Take care. I love you.

Stacey

Devon frowned as she reread Stacey's e-mail. She had something that she needed to talk to her about? What on earth could that mean? As her eyes scrolled to the last question she couldn't help but smile as she hit the reply tab on the open window.

Hey Stace-

I'm writing you from her cabin! Working like a dog, but I now have a standing invite for dinner and a shower and...you fill in the rest. And before you ask, because I know you will, yes, the sex is still amazing. In fact, I have yet to find anything about her that isn't amazing. I'll have to tell you more later.

Please don't make me worry, just tell me what you need to talk to me about.

I love you,

Dev

Devon absentmindedly pulled another mint leaf from her bag as she set her laptop aside. For a moment she was content just to watch Elaine chew on her lip as she studied the book in her hands. Elaine sitting there in her boxers and tank top was much too tempting. Devon's heart skipped and she had no idea how this woman had such power over her. Before she even realized she was moving, Devon was across the room. Without a word she found Elaine's hand and gave it a gentle tug. Elaine's eyes met hers and Devon was helpless to look away as she led them both across the room and to bed.

In the early morning light, Elaine watched as Devon slept. She had spent the last several days searching for signs of the poachers while Devon continued her research. In the evenings, they would each work. Elaine completed her reports while Devon documented her research. When Elaine finished her own work she helped Devon sift through the piles of data that she had collected. Devon was exceedingly pleased and grateful that Elaine was willing and capable of helping her. Once work was done, they would share dinner, a shower and hours of lovemaking.

It had been idyllic. And now it was almost over. Real life was waiting.

In the early light of dawn it was easy for Elaine to imagine waking up with Devon every day. She was beautiful and Elaine loved waking her with gentle kisses and caresses. Thoughts of parting made Elaine's heart ache and for a while it was easy to think it would all work out somehow, dating when they both went home, being together enough even when new assignments would call them both away for months at a time.

Devon's departure was imminent—she had maybe three or four days of research left. Elaine could be leaving as early as then provided they found the poachers or no more reports of slaughtered animals came in.

The future was rushing at them. She worried that neither of them could talk about it. It was too much, too soon, too risky—when their time here in this cabin was so very simple. But the bottom line was Elaine couldn't imagine not seeing Devon again. Something would have to work out.

Chapter 14

"Hey, Elaine, are you there?" A burst of static followed.

Damn! Elaine jumped out of bed and hurried across the cold floor to the radio.

"Yeah, Brad. Go ahead."

"Donovan is in the lower basin and heard shots. He could probably use some backup."

"Tell him I'm on my way."

Devon shifted and sat on the edge of the bed. She stretched and Elaine tore her gaze from the alluring sight. Shots fired meant no good, least of all for Donovan.

"I should probably be heading out, too."

Elaine gently pushed Devon back onto the bed. "Please don't go back to your camp today. This has got to be the poachers and these people are stupid, scared and armed. I need to make sure you will be out of harm's way."

"But..."

"Please, Devon?"

Devon wanted to argue but the look in Elaine's eyes convinced her and she nodded in agreement.

Elaine quickly dressed and motioned toward the radio. "I'll let you know when I'm on my way back."

"Be careful." Devon's strained gaze strayed to Elaine's rifle. "Please be careful."

"I always am." Elaine gave her a reassuring smile as she strapped on her belt and gun. "Go back to sleep." Elaine flashed a cocky grin as she grabbed the rifle next to the door and headed out without another word.

It didn't take Elaine long to reach Donovan, though her bones felt jolted by the pace she'd driven over the snow, slush and mud-choked roads.

"Hey Cap! How was the drive down?"

"Pretty good. What do we have?"

"Bear shot over in the field. It's definitely a fresh kill."

"A bear out this early?"

Donovan shrugged, looking as perplexed as she felt.

"Any sign of the shooter?"

"No, it looks like maybe they've cleared out."

"Keep your eyes open. We can't be too careful."

Donovan nodded. "Yes, ma'am."

Elaine slung her rifle over her shoulder. "Let's take a look."

He led her to the bear that had been killed and was left where it had fallen. The sight of the dead animal made her sick. She just couldn't imagine why someone would shoot this magnificent creature for sport. Many poachers killed the wildlife because they were after the fur or something else the animal had to offer, but these kills seemed pointless. They had taken nothing, skinned nothing; simply killed the innocent animal and moved on.

Judging by the way the bear had fallen they figured the

poachers had probably shot from the north tree line. Not wanting to be surprised by the hunters, she and Donovan split up, staying in visual range of each other. Elaine doubted they would still be at the edge of the clearing, but she wasn't willing to take any chances. They headed toward the trees, thankful the poachers weren't able to hide their boot prints in the remaining snow.

With the exchange of a look Elaine and Donovan both removed their rifles from their shoulders, carrying them instead barrel down. Elaine motioned for Donovan to stay to the trees and stay alert. They both knew the drill. They had been trained in similar scenarios and this wasn't the first time either of them had to deal with the real thing.

They were well into the woods when another shot rang out. The sound reverberated around them and Elaine knew the hunters were just ahead of them. She motioned for Donovan to stop moving while she listened. It sounded as though there were two, maybe three men laughing. *Fuck.*

The men continued to laugh and brag about the animal they had taken down. Their boisterous cheering made it easy for the rangers to zero in on them. Between the trees, Elaine could see three men. The first was tall and thin with scraggly blond hair and looked to be in his mid-twenties. The second was short, stout, with gray hair that made him appear older than his counterparts. The third was rather large, easily six feet tall, with broad shoulders and dark hair and seemed more intoxicated than the other two. None of them looked as if they had bathed in weeks.

They took their positions based on the lay of the land. Donovan kneeled in the snow behind a large rock with his rifle cocked and aimed. Elaine took a defensive stance, shielded by a tree; rifle aimed, ready to pull the trigger if necessary.

The three hunters held their rifles loosely. Elaine watched as they stumbled and swayed, each using the other for support. Their speech was slurred and she wondered just how much they had drunk. It was amazing the bear hadn't gotten them first—and if it had she'd have cheered. They deserved worse. It's one thing to take down an idiot with a gun, but it was even harder to take down three, especially when they were drunk and their already bad judgment was impaired. The situation was unpredictable at best and could definitely be life threatening. *Fuck me! This isn't going to be easy. Fuck! Fuck! Fuck!*

She could feel the adrenaline surging through her veins. She quelled the tremor in her arms. This was what practice was all about. She signaled to Donovan before firmly and clearly commanding, "Put your rifles on the ground and place your hands on your heads. Now!"

Two of the men quickly did as she instructed. The large dark-haired man, with flask in hand, swung around and raised his rifle.

It was as if it all happened in slow motion. As he turned, he raised his rifle directly at Elaine. He pulled the trigger just as Donovan fired. Elaine darted behind the tree as she felt bits of bark ricochet off her cheek and she turned her face away from the flying debris. *That was way too close.*

Donovan's shot had only been a flesh wound to the thigh, but it was enough to get the shooter to lay down his gun. Within moments they had all three men on their knees, hands cuffed behind their backs.

As Elaine collected their rifles, Donovan saw blood on Elaine's sleeve.

"Cap, you okay?" He motioned with his head to her arm. She looked at her arm and was surprised to find a small patch of blood. "Yeah. I didn't even notice, probably just a scratch."

The bastard who had taken the shot at her was whimpering about his leg, which was hardly bleeding. She thought about the bear, the deer and all the other animals they had killed and could barely resist the urge to kick him square in his wound. It would have been easier to resist if he hadn't just shot at her.

Donovan saw her clenched jaw and flashed her a smile. "Wish you'd shot him?"

Elaine grinned. "If I'd shot him, it wouldn't have been a flesh wound."

Donovan shrugged. "I didn't want to have to carry his sorry ass out of here."

She turned to the younger blond-haired man and asked, "How many animals have you killed?"

The idiot shrugged. "I dunno. Who can remember?"

Elaine turned her attention to the trigger-happy idiot. She wasn't sure whether the shot he had fired had been deliberate or just the result of being shit-faced drunk, but either way, he'd now have to pay the price. "We definitely have you on two federal counts. Do you think we won't press charges?"

The bastard slurred, "I know my rights."

Elaine's smile was cold. "So you know that you will be tried in a federal court for your actions? This is federal land. And you shot at a federal officer. That would be me."

The older man looked a bit squeamish. "Fuck, Joe. You didn't say this was federal land. We were just supposed to be having some fun."

"Both of you just shut the hell up."

The younger man spoke up, clearly shaken. "You damn near shot that person over on the river, Joe."

Elaine's blood felt like it froze in her veins. *Had they seen Devon? What would they have done if they would have figured out she was a woman? A woman who didn't carry a gun?*

"Shut the fuck up, Roy!"

Elaine looked at Donovan before turning to Joe. She held his eyes and crouched down in front of him. Her voice was low and intense. "Be thankful I wasn't the one who pulled the trigger. You wouldn't be walking out of here, but you would be very much alive." Her eyes burned with anger and her voice lowered to an icy whisper that was meant for his ears only. "I would have left your sorry ass out here covered in fresh blood and let the animals have their way with you." Elaine's words were spoken softly but the man quickly pulled away from her, the blood draining from his face.

She finally turned back to Donovan. "Let's get them out of here."

They led the men back out of the clearing to Donovan's SUV. They secured the hunters' weapons in the cab and put the three men in the back behind the cage. The poachers would be taken back to the station and processed for illegally hunting on federal land. Joe had earned himself a special charge of attempted murder for the shot he fired at Elaine. She was relieved that these three men would be thinking about their actions in a prison cell for many years to come. The gratification she felt at having stopped any more senseless killings was just another reason why she loved her job.

"What did you say to him back there?"

Elaine smiled. "Just told him that it wasn't nice to pull a gun on a lady."

Donovan looked at her for a long minute before nodding. Elaine hadn't done anything illegal, but he probably didn't want to know what all was said. Neither wanted him to have to lie in court to protect his captain.

"Are you going to ride with me back to the station, Cap?"

"Yeah. I'll just need you to bring me back to my truck once we wrap this up."

"Yes, ma'am."

As she opened the door to climb inside the SUV, her mind filled with all the things that could have happened if the bastards had found Devon…alone. The thought of the three idiots coming across anyone was frightening, but she tried to convince herself that they had *not* come across Devon. But what if?

En route to the station, Donovan radioed in that there was a ranger in need of medical attention and the poachers were in custody. Elaine wanted to contact Devon and let her know she would be held up at the station and would be back as soon as possible, but doing that in front of an audience wasn't exactly what she had in mind.

As soon as they arrived at the station, her crew was waiting outside with an ambulance. The relief on their faces was apparent and Elaine was touched that they had obviously been so worried. Over the next few hours, they finished their statements regarding the shooting and subsequent arrests, but not before she was checked out by emergency services.

It wasn't until the medic began cutting away her bloody shirt that she realized she had been grazed by the bullet that the drunken moron had fired her way. Only then did it begin to sting. The medic reassured her that it wasn't anything to worry about, but instructed her to keep it clean and dressed to avoid infection. She couldn't help but notice that it would probably leave a nice scar.

Elaine was beat by the time she parked her truck outside of the cabin. Dealing with three drunken buffoons and a bear carcass, plus the roundtrip to the station and pages of paperwork had taken a mental and emotional toll on her. Elaine glanced again at the supplies that she loaded up before leaving the station. She knew that she should carry them in, but they would keep till morning. As tired as she was, she wasn't going to wait a moment longer to see Devon.

Chapter 15

Devon wanted to know who Elaine was kidding. How was she supposed to go back to sleep knowing that Elaine was heading in the direction of gunfire?

She crawled from the bed and headed for the shower. She stood relaxing under the hot water, letting it gradually awaken her. The heat helped to clear her mind. She toweled herself dry and wiped the steam from the mirror and then brushed her teeth and dressed while she thought about Elaine.

She glanced at her watch and saw that Elaine had only been gone thirty minutes. This promised to be a long day. She wasn't a fool; of course she was going to worry about Elaine.

Suddenly her thoughts gravitated to her brother-in-law. He was in a war zone every day and every day her sister believed in her husband. Like Phillip, Elaine was a professional. Yes, things could go wrong, but spending her day worrying about it wouldn't change anything. Devon focused on the fact that Elaine was not only a ranger but she was a captain—a captain with many years experience and damn good at her job. If Raine was able to cope day in and day out with her husband doing his job, then surely she could handle this. She trusted Elaine and knew that she wouldn't take any unnecessary risks.

Devon booted up her laptop and was pleased that it was a little faster today. With the storms having cleared out and the added advantage of being at the top of the ridge, her signal was stronger and faster, even if she did feel like she was still in the days of slow modem dial-ups. It beat the hell out of the service she had a few days ago.

She quickly scanned the e-mails from her sister and Stacey to ensure that Raine was all right. After learning that all was well, she decided to respond to those later. She really needed to get some work done first. She had been sending in her daily field notes, but she needed to generate some more detailed reports for study and analysis.

She set up a number of sample slides and placed them under the microscope, noting where each was pulled from and when. After looking at each and labeling them with location, species and date, she tucked them into the insulated kit that she would use to transport them back to the lab. She spent the next several hours poring over slides and research and developing flow charts and graphs that she e-mailed to her lab. She completed a series of reports detailing the progress that had been made with the planting and regrowth in the area and sent copies to all appropriate department heads. Even with the time she had spent with Elaine she was still on track to make it back in time for Raine's delivery date.

Devon's organizational skills and her almost anal need to do things in an orderly and timely fashion had helped keep her on track thus far. Although her fear for Elaine's safety lurked in the back of her mind, she chose to put her faith in Elaine and her abilities to do her job. Knowing that Elaine was a smart and competent ranger helped ease Devon's worries and allowed her to concentrate on her work. Not to mention, she hoped that the reported gunfire meant Elaine would finally catch the poachers that had been killing innocent animals for months now. She knew how important it was to Elaine to catch the assholes and Devon herself was looking forward to seeing them face criminal charges.

After completing her first round of duties, she started on the next batch. Within a few hours she had sifted through all of her slides, logged and recorded each one and had filled out the proper paperwork and sent it in. She probably could have been finished sooner except her computer connection was still slow. Her thoughts turned to Elaine as she caught sight of the radio. In spite of her concern, she had managed to complete a lot of work.

After she hit the send button on her last e-mail which detailed the transformation and rejuvenation of the flora along the riverbank, with accompanying pictures, she waited patiently for the e-mail to upload. Once completed, she reopened her sister's e-mail.

She couldn't help but be amused. Raine bitched relentlessly about how protective Stacey was and if she didn't know better she would think that Stacey was the father. When Raine had voiced the same frustrations to Phillip, he had proudly announced that he had already talked to Stacey and they both agreed this was the best form of care for Raine. So Raine, having failed with both Stacey and her own husband, was appealing to her older sister to get Stacey to quit being quite *so* attentive. Devon knew it would be pointless to address the issue with Stacey. Once Stacey had her mind set on something, nobody could change it. Absolutely nobody. Not even her best friend. In spite of that fact she dutifully informed her sister that she would *try*.

In the middle of her e-mail she heard the echo of a very distant gunshot. In a nanosecond her worry for Elaine went from back-of-her-mind to front and center. She said a silent prayer for Elaine's safe return. She paused for a moment and thought about what Raine had said about Phillip being in the middle of a war-torn country. She had always said that if something were wrong she would feel it and each day she didn't feel that anything was wrong so she was able to get through it. Of course, there was the baby to think about now and Raine didn't have much choice but to get through each day. But she still maintained that she and Phillip were connected on such a level that she would know if something had happened to him.

Devon didn't know that she was on that level with Elaine yet. Obviously they had great chemistry in and out of bed and they could talk for hours or not at all. But did that mean that she would know if something had happened to Elaine? Devon's logical thought process told her that if the situation was reversed and it was her out there, she wouldn't want Elaine to worry about her. She would want Elaine to trust in her. Yes, a healthy amount of concern was good but she wasn't going to doubt Elaine's ability to do her job and do it well. So she offered up yet another prayer before picking up her cell phone. She needed a distraction and the ear of a best friend.

Stacey answered on the second ring.

"Dev?"

"Hey." Devon was amazed and pleased that there was very little static compared to the last time they talked.

Devon smiled as Stacey cut to the chase. "Raine is doing well. I'm fine. What's wrong?"

"What's wrong is that you leave me a cryptic e-mail saying that we need to talk and then follow it up with nothing. Plus, I have Raine complaining that you are smothering her and driving her absolutely batty."

"So did something happen with you and Elaine?"

"No, nothing happened with Elaine. She's off playing ranger. Now quit avoiding the topics at hand. What is the news you need to talk to me about and will you please cut Raine a little slack?"

Stacey laughed. "I'm just doing as her husband asked. But yes, I will cut her a little slack. I will let her reach to the middle rows in the aisles at the grocery store to lift things that weigh three pounds or less."

Devon couldn't help but laugh. God she knew how Stacey could be and if it was truly this bad it was no wonder Raine was complaining. Not that she really thought Phillip would be any different. "You better be careful Stace or she'll ditch you."

Stacey laughed wickedly. "She can't. Even when I don't have her house staked out, I put a GPS on her car and she has no idea." There was a long pause. "And it had better stay that way."

Devon laughed hysterically. This was exactly what she needed. "I won't tell on you but only if you tell me what it was you needed to talk to me about."

Stacey sighed. "I seem to be in a bit of a pickle."

"Stacey Bailey! What have you done?"

Stacey laughed. "Why is it that you assume I'm the one who did something?"

"Because I know you."

Stacey let out a slow breath. "Well, I'm not really sure that I've done anything. Hell, I don't even know how to explain."

"Why don't you just start at the beginning?"

"Okay. I had the most amazing sex of my life."

Devon asked slowly, "And?"

"And nothing. She won't even acknowledge it or me for that matter."

"What?"

Stacey's laughter held no mirth. "For the first time in my life, I want to sleep with someone more than once. It was far beyond amazing. I want more than just one night and she doesn't want me."

Devon was incredulous. *No one* had ever *not* wanted to sleep with Stacey a second time. She always seemed to have the opposite problem. Once she slept with a woman, she couldn't get rid of her. Not only was it extraordinary that a woman would reject Stacey, it was just as amazing that Stacey wanted more than just one night. It wasn't that Stacey had never slept with the same woman twice; it was just that she didn't consider it very sporting.

"Stacey, I have a very hard time believing that."

"Believe it, love. It's true."

"Stace…"

"Hey Dev, I need to go. That's Raine on the other line."

"Okay. But don't consider this conversation over." She warned before saying a quick, "I love you. 'Bye."

"I love you too. 'Bye."

Devon sat holding her phone for a few minutes. She and Stacey had an agreement that no matter what they were talking about, it could wait if Raine called. She knew that Stacey would call her back immediately if there was a problem.

But that wasn't what gave Devon pause. She had never thought she would hear Stacey say that there was a woman that she *wanted*. Something about Stacey's voice told Devon that this was different. This woman was different than anyone Stacey had ever encountered before. This wasn't about the challenge. Whoever this mystery woman was, she had gotten to Stacey.

Devon understood the feeling. Elaine had gotten under her skin. She hadn't even seen it coming and Devon suspected that Stacey was about to be in a very similar position.

It had seemed like hours when Devon finally heard the static from the radio echo throughout the cabin. She jumped at the unexpected sound and rose from the couch to listen, hoping beyond hope that it was Elaine and she was just letting her know she was on her way back.

"Anyone copy?" Devon could hear a man's voice dripping with what she interpreted as tension.

A second disembodied voice answered, "Go ahead."

"This is Donovan. We are on our way back with three suspects in custody. We have a wounded ranger. ETA is twenty minutes."

"Copy that. We'll have a medic waiting."

A wounded ranger? Medic?

Devon's heart raced as she took in the information. It had to be Elaine. She sat at the table in the kitchen area tapping her fingers...waiting. It was suddenly just too much to sit still. She paced, willed the radio to bring her some news. But it remained silent.

Elaine hadn't even closed the truck door when Devon appeared at the top of the steps. Devon's face was drawn and she stood with her arms crossed across her chest.

"Are you okay? The radio said you were hurt. Why didn't you let me know you were okay?"

The words fell in a jumble all around her. She realized Devon was in tears. "Honey, I'm so sorry you were worried," she said as she hurried up the stairs.

She was pulled into Devon's arms. Devon's lips found hers and Elaine pulled her into a fierce embrace for a long, deep kiss. Devon pressed closer to the strong body that held her. They finally pulled apart laboring for breath.

"Does that mean you missed me?"

"You know I did."

She slipped out of her jacket as she said, "I'm still in one piece. There was nothing to worry about."

The look on Devon's face grew from one of relief to one of concern. "Your arm."

Elaine followed the path of Devon's gaze.

Just beneath the T-shirt she had slipped on, her bandage was noticeable. She mentally scolded herself for not having chosen a long sleeve shirt rather than just accepting what had been offered. But she had been in a hurry and pulled on the offered shirt after the paramedic had annihilated the sleeve of her uniform.

"It's okay; just a little scratch."

"Just a scratch? Ever since I heard the radio transmission, I've been worried sick. Does this happen often?"

"No." Elaine hoped her expression was warm and reassuring.

Devon gave her a look of disbelief. "I saw the other scars on your body. I guess I really didn't want to think about how you got them."

She simply shrugged and wrapped Devon in her arms again. "Really, I'm okay. And I'm sorry for not calling you. We had to transport the poachers to the station and then there was all the paperwork..."

"And the medic," Devon interrupted.

"Yes. That too, but I just got grazed. I promise I am fine, really."

"I can't stand thinking about you getting hurt."

"I appreciate that. I don't like thinking about me getting hurt either." She grinned.

Devon caressed her cheek. "Why don't you put on something more comfortable?" With a wink and a smile to lighten the mood she asked, "Would you like me to get your bear slippers?"

She couldn't help but laugh. Leave it to Devon to make her laugh, even when her eyes were red from tears and worry.

"Would you like something to eat? I saved you some dinner."

"I had something at the station." She began putting her jacket on but Devon stopped her.

"What are you doing?"

"I left some supplies in the truck and I'm going out to get them." She winced as she attempted to put on her jacket.

"You'll do no such thing. You can sit here and rest. I'll go get them." She was back in just moments, kicking the door open with her foot and setting the chest in a chair. "Just what in the world are you doing?"

Elaine looked up from the coffee she was preparing. "What?"

"You need to take it easy. Sit!" Devon commanded.

She reluctantly obeyed.

"I'm not helpless, you know?"

"I am fully aware of that, but you are injured. Did they give you some painkillers? And there is nothing wrong with letting me take care of you." Without another word, Devon turned to finish preparing the coffee.

She settled at the table, noting that Devon's microscope and laptop had obviously been in use. She could feel the knots forming in her shoulders and she rolled them trying to loosen them up. She sighed when strong hands settled on her shoulders and gently massaged.

"That feels so good."

Elaine could feel the familiar roller coaster in her stomach as she leaned her head back against firm full breasts. Devon continued to work her shoulders before moving her hands to her neck. Elaine groaned and dropped her head forward letting those magic fingers work on her sore muscles.

She was thoroughly relaxed when Devon gave her shoulders one last squeeze before stepping away.

Devon cleared their cups and cleaned the kitchen. As she wrung out the towel and reached to hang it, she felt Elaine's arms slide around her. She leaned back against Elaine's warm body.

Turning in Elaine's arms, she kissed her gently. Elaine's hands were sure on her body. Every time she touched this woman she wanted to make love to her. But between Elaine's wound and the fatigue clearly visible on her face she knew there would be no lovemaking tonight. Her own emotions were too raw from worry. As much as she wanted Elaine she was just as content with the thought of holding her as they slept.

"Can we talk?" Elaine asked.

"Of course."

Devon led her to the couch where she directed Elaine to lay with her head in Devon's lap. She ran her fingers through Elaine's hair and felt a quiver in the pit of her stomach at Elaine's appreciative moan. She continued her ministrations while she waited for Elaine to voice whatever was on her mind.

"I know that you only have a couple of more days up here and now that we have taken care of our poacher problem I won't be staying any longer either."

Devon leaned down and placed a leisurely kiss on Elaine's lips. "Uh-huh?"

"And I was thinking…Well, I was wondering…"

Devon continued to run her fingers through Elaine's hair, not sure which one of them enjoyed the sensation more. "What were you wondering?"

Elaine was silent for a long moment. "I guess I was wondering if maybe when we leave here if maybe you would consider seeing me again."

Devon was thrilled that Elaine wanted to continue seeing her and had to rein in the butterflies in her stomach so that she would speak coherently. "Hmm…when do you have to report back in to the station?"

Elaine's brow furrowed in confusion. "Well I need to e-mail in a field report when I get back but then I'll have a couple of days off before I have to return to work and fill out what will no doubt be a mountain of reports and forms that have piled up. Probably have to give an interview to prosecution and defense for those asshole poachers."

Devon grinned. "In that case I would imagine that the next time we see each other will be when we leave these mountains and you follow me home to spend the night with me." She paused. "Unless, of course, you need to go straight home."

Elaine laughed. "There's nothing that can't wait a little longer."

She eased herself up from under Elaine and then held out her hand to help her up off the sofa.

Elaine lurched slightly and fished a bottle out of her pocket. "I think I will have a couple of these. I'm so stiff."

She steered her toward the bed. "I'll get you some water. You get comfy. Take all the pillows you need."

"Yes ma'am."

She helped Elaine out of her clothes, then fetched water before stripping and joining Elaine under the blankets. She pulled Elaine into her arms and simply held her. They might not be making love tonight but the feeling of Elaine in her arms was just as comforting.

Chapter 16

Devon stood on the deck chewing on a mint leaf as she looked out over the canyon. Her hair was still damp from her shower. Elaine had closed up everything beneath the cabin while she bathed. She was now in the shower and Devon took the opportunity to enjoy the peace of the woodlands below and reflect on her time here.

Elaine had helped her finish gathering her samples and packing them for travel. Together they had broken down her camp the night before and lugged everything up the mountain. That way Elaine could drive Devon to her truck in the morning without having to make any stops. She was pleased that not only would she not have to hike all of her gear out but she would be able to spend more time with Elaine.

They had risen early and packed all their gear into Elaine's truck before showering. As it was she was glad that after having worked up a sweat she was clean and wouldn't have to smell herself on the drive home.

She thought about the many conversations they had shared over evening meals. She was profoundly grateful that Elaine had said that her emotional ties with Grace had been over for a long time, long enough that Devon had no substantial fears of being the rebound woman.

She was still lost in thought when she felt Elaine's arms wrap around her. Even now, fully dressed, the sensation awakened every nerve in her body. Elaine had slipped on loose jeans and a sweatshirt. In uniform or casually dressed, Elaine was the sexiest woman Devon had ever laid eyes on.

As her head rested against Elaine's chest she thought again about Elaine and Grace's relationship. She couldn't imagine ever having a relationship that resembled theirs. After the things Elaine had shared about Grace she could easily see why Elaine had begun a relationship with Grace. Grace had represented herself to be everything that Elaine wanted in a partner. Hell, the woman was already in the forest service so why wouldn't Elaine think that they would want the same thing?

And she could see now why Elaine had let the relationship continue. Elaine naturally saw the good in people and was hopeful and optimistic that her relationship with Grace would improve and ultimately survive, but apparently Grace hadn't had that goal at all. She vowed that the trust Elaine had placed in her would *not*, would *never* be shattered. It had taken time, but Elaine had eventually opened up and shared many details about Grace. She had the feeling that talking about it had been cathartic for Elaine.

Elaine's voice was quiet next to her ear. "Are you all right?"

She was *not* going to let thoughts of Grace affect their last morning together in this paradise. "Yes. I was just thinking about how much I'm going to miss this place."

Elaine held up the keys to the cabin. "There is nothing to say that we can't come back."

She turned in Elaine's arms. "You would want to come back

here?"

Elaine dropped a tender kiss on Devon's lips. "Yes. I would. This place holds some special memories."

She wrapped her arms around Elaine and rested her head on her shoulder. "Yes, it does, doesn't it?"

"Are you ready to leave?"

Devon stepped out of Elaine's arms and sighed. "Not really, but I guess it's that time isn't it?"

If she didn't need to get home before Raine went into labor and have work to attend to, Devon would have happily stayed several more weeks. She gave the cabin one last, longing look.

Elaine locked up the cabin and checked all the details one last time. The generator was secure. The pile of firewood was restocked and the cabin door was sealed. Once she was satisfied that she hadn't forgotten anything, she walked to her truck where Devon sat waiting.

She climbed in and Devon leaned across the seat for a long kiss before she could even get the truck started. It was a few minutes before seat belts were fastened and she put the truck into gear.

Grace, I never thought I would be thanking you for anything ever again. But if you hadn't done what you did then I wouldn't have been so eager to take this assignment and I would have never met the most wonderful woman in the world.

Devon reached across the seat for Elaine's hand. The touch sent familiar electricity up her arm. She didn't even have to question if Devon's touch would always do this to her. She knew without a doubt that, God willing, fifty years from now, it would.

"Are you looking forward to going to your house?" Devon asked.

Elaine shrugged. She hadn't really thought about it. There was nothing there that she wanted to go home to. Brad would

157

continue to stop in and water her plants. Outside of that she really had no reason to go back to her house. Especially since that was all that it was, a house. Not a home.

Elaine shrugged. "I have to do laundry."

Devon smiled. "I do own a washer and dryer, you know?"

As they pulled to a stop next to Devon's Toyota, she unbuckled her seat belt and leaned over to give Elaine another long, lingering kiss.

Pleasantly lightheaded, Elaine suggested, "Why don't you go ahead and leave your stuff in the back of my truck? That way we don't have to move it now. It can wait until we get to your place."

Devon smiled. "Sounds like a plan," she said before she slipped out of the forestry truck and located the keys to her own.

Elaine waited for Devon to get her truck started and warmed up and then pulled out and followed Devon back to the main road and into town. She felt a little giddy, almost like a school girl, at the prospect of seeing Devon's house and sharing her bed tonight.

Devon found her gaze torn between the road ahead of her and Elaine's headlights in the rearview mirror. A few weeks ago she had headed into the mountains, certain she had nothing to look forward to but long days of work. Instead her life had changed. She smiled at the thought of Elaine sleeping in *her* bed, in *her* home. She still wasn't ready to tell Elaine that she loved her, although she was certain of her feelings. She thought perhaps they might need some time together away from the mountains and the cabin. Time to acclimate to civilization...together.

She was looking forward to introducing Elaine to Raine and Stacey. She knew that they would like her. "What isn't there to like?" she asked the steering wheel.

She reached onto the passenger seat and found her phone and Bluetooth. She left a short message for Raine letting her know that she was exhausted and on her way home. She also conveyed that she loved her and would see her soon. While part of her was torn between her desire to see Stacey and Raine she really just wanted to spend the evening alone with Elaine. As she dialed Stacey's number, she glanced into the mirror once again to make sure that she hadn't lost Elaine.

"Hey, Stace."

"Dev, love, how are you? All is well here."

"I'm good. Very good, actually. I'm on my way home."

"That's terrific news. We've missed you terribly and can't wait to see you."

"Me too. I *am* on my way home, but I'm not alone. I have a favor to ask."

"Hmm. I see. What do you need? Anything for you."

"Elaine is following me back to my house. Would you mind going to the market and bringing some fresh groceries to the house? I'd love to make her dinner later."

"You got it."

"Thanks, Stace. I appreciate it. I will call you tomorrow."

"All right, love. Don't do anything I wouldn't do."

That detail taken care of, she oriented herself in her week's schedule. It was Thursday and they wouldn't get back until late. She would have to drop her samples by the lab tomorrow, but didn't actually have to return to work until Monday. She wondered how Elaine would feel about meeting Raine and Stacey. Was it too soon to introduce Elaine to her family? It didn't feel like it.

She normally didn't bring women into her home, but Elaine wasn't just any woman. The thought of having Elaine there felt so right, she had no reservations at all. *Jesus, how does she make me feel this way?*

Chapter 17

Devon had no sooner set her backpack down when she was pulled into Elaine's strong arms. Elaine's kiss was urgent as she found Devon's mouth. Devon's hands slipped down to Elaine's hips pulling their bodies closer together. The drive had seemed like an eternity. She was vaguely aware of the door being kicked shut and her back being pressed against the wall, but after that, there was only Elaine.

Elaine finally pulled away. "You can't kiss me like you did back there, get me all hot and leave me wanting you the entire drive back."

Devon lifted a finger and traced Elaine's jaw. "Of course I can."

"You don't play fair."

Devon laughed. "And you're just now figuring this out?"

Elaine lowered her mouth next to Devon's ear. "I don't intend to play fair tonight."

It was several hours later when they were both satiated, their bodies still entwined that Devon languidly asked, "Would you like some dinner?"

"I'm not sure."

Devon arched a brow. "You don't know if you're hungry?"

Elaine laughed. "Were you planning on us going out or calling something in?"

Devon smiled. "I thought I might cook for you."

"Well, I know my fridge only has spoiled milk in it at this point. What did you have in mind?"

Devon laughed at the skeptical look in Elaine's eyes as she found a shirt. They padded down the hall into the kitchen in their stocking feet. Devon flipped on the kitchen light and moved to the fridge to see what Stacey had bought.

"Would you like some help?"

"That depends. Do you want something fancy or something simple?"

Elaine's brow arched suggestively. "I think simple would be good, I don't know how long I'm willing to let you stay out of bed."

Devon laughed. "Let me? And here I was thinking I was being a good hostess by letting you out of bed."

"I thought *you* were hungry." Elaine poked her playfully in the stomach.

Elaine's stomach growled and Devon laughed. "It would seem you worked up an appetite as well."

Devon produced some fresh veggies for a salad and put some water on to boil fettuccine. As the kitchen filled with the smell of garlic and onion, Elaine looked around Devon's house. She hadn't had much time to notice anything before as they had made it to Devon's bedroom so quickly.

"You have a nice house."

"Thanks. I call it home." Devon smiled appreciatively.

As she stirred the pasta, Devon felt a strong arm wrap around her and she leaned back into Elaine's body. She loved the way that Elaine would stand behind her, her arms wrapped gently but securely around her. She also liked the fact that Elaine seemed to have an equally hard time keeping her hands off Devon's body. When Elaine touched her or looked at her she felt like the most exquisite woman in the world. And when Elaine told her she was beautiful, she believed it wholeheartedly. She wanted nothing more than to make Elaine feel the same.

"Are you sure you don't need any help?" Elaine whispered in her ear before moving her lips to Devon's neck.

"Mmm…if you keep doing that, I may burn dinner."

Elaine swiped a carrot and was busily chewing on it as she studied the small wine rack. "Can I at least open some wine?"

"Sure. This will be done in just a few more minutes. Corkscrew is in the drawer on the end."

"The longer that cooks, the hungrier I get."

A few minutes later Devon dished out the pasta and set it on the breakfast bar with the salad. Elaine devoured every bite. Devon loved sitting across the bar from Elaine. It felt so right.

When Elaine finally pushed her dishes aside, she asked, "How is it that you were gone for so long and come home to fresh vegetables?"

"I may have called a friend and explained that I was hoping to seduce this really hot ranger with a hot meal."

Devon had turned back to washing when she suddenly felt Elaine's breath on her neck. "How hot was this ranger?"

Devon set the bowl she was washing in the dishwasher, rinsed her hands and dried them before she turned into Elaine's arms. "Hot enough that I had to bring her home with me."

Soft gentle kisses moved ever so slowly down to the rapid pulse at the base of Devon's neck. "Hmm. Maybe you should show me again how hot this ranger is while I peel that adorable shirt off of you."

"Again? I thought you would have had enough of me by now," Devon teased.

"I'll never get enough of you," Elaine whispered, sending a

shiver the length of Devon's body.

"Good morning," Elaine said lazily as she joined Devon in the shower. "Or should I say afternoon? Sorry I'm such a sleepyhead."

"Like I didn't just get up myself."

They kissed tenderly as they washed each other. One thing led to another until the hot water abruptly turned icy.

"It's exhilarating to swim in a cold river, but I never feel the same way about a cold shower," Elaine said as she dried Devon's back.

"My fault. I threw a load of clothes in the washer. Do you need something to wear until the clean stuff is dry?"

"Well, given that what I had left that was clean is still out in the truck, sure. It's a little early to shock the neighbors."

Devon laughed and went to find some shorts and a Tee. After that, food was a priority.

When they were finished eating brunch, Devon finally asked, "Would you like a tour of the house?"

Elaine smiled. "We kind of skipped over that part didn't we?"

Devon's only response was a gentle laugh. She cleared the dishes from the counter, placing them in the dishwasher. She pulled a fresh mint leaf from the plant on the windowsill and placed it on her tongue before coming around to take Elaine's hand.

"You know for the longest time I couldn't figure out how your kisses always tasted so minty. Actually your *entire* body tastes like mint. I finally saw you chewing on those things."

"Every part of my body?"

Elaine nodded.

"Does it bother you?" Devon asked. She had never had anyone tell her that the mint leaves she so enjoyed eating permeated her entire body. It was an amazing feeling knowing that Elaine had noticed how every inch of her skin tasted. She had never even considered that even her most inner parts would taste of mint.

"Not at all."

"Would you like one?"

"Umm…no."

The dubious expression on Elaine's face amused Devon. It was one that Devon was used to seeing. Most people thought she was a bit wacky because she chewed on mint leaves rather than gum or breath mints. But she figured as far as vices went hers wasn't that bad. "I'm addicted to the things. Always have been since I was a kid."

She tugged gently on Elaine's hand pulling her to her feet. "You've seen the kitchen and the glamorous breakfast bar. The living room we'll get to. The bedroom you've sort of seen." She gestured and Elaine grinned. "This is where I really live."

Devon led her back down the hall, past the spare bathroom and bedroom. The door opposite of the master bedroom opened to a study. Two of the walls were floor to ceiling glass windows that overlooked beautiful fields of wildflowers. A wooden framed glass door opened onto an inviting deck that stretched the entire back of the house. A large built-in bookshelf made up the remaining wall with a small potbellied stove in the corner. There was a large overstuffed chair in one corner sitting with a lamp and an end table. The only clutter in the room was on the desk. Folders and paperwork were strewn across the surface and the chair was well worn. She crossed to the plant rack. "Stacey's done a good job with these. I kill houseplants. It's really sad."

"This is Raine and Phillip's wedding?" Elaine picked up one of the photos tucked among the books.

"Yeah." Devon touched another frame, tracing her mother's smile. "These are my parents." She pointed to a smiling man and woman standing on either side of Devon who was sporting a graduation cap and gown. She felt Elaine give her hand a gentle squeeze.

"Family reunion?" Elaine pointed to an older photo

containing a group of at least two dozen adults and kids. After Devon nodded, she added, "Nobody's crying or sulking?"

Devon shrugged. "The ones that did we threw in the lake." She was pleased when Elaine laughed. "Let's get some coffee and go out on the deck."

From the kitchen the deck was easily accessed by the French doors out of the living room. Devon led Elaine out onto the deck saying, "This is the most peaceful place in my life." *Well, it used to be. Now your arms are the most peaceful place I can imagine ever being.*

The wooden deck overlooked a secluded backyard with a pool and a beautiful grassy area that was framed by an amazing field of early spring wildflowers. Just beyond the field, the hill and trees gave way to a magnificent view of the valley beyond. Off in the distance between the foothills, Elaine caught sight of an array of flora in all its glory.

"Aren't you worried that someone will buy the property around you and build on it?"

Devon turned and smiled at her as she pulled Elaine closer to her. "I probably would be if I didn't own it."

Elaine's eyebrows shot up as she looked at Devon. "Clearly I'm in the wrong line of work."

Devon laughed. "When I bought the property there was nothing around here. The only way I could get to it was down a dusty one-lane gravel road. I hadn't planned on buying much more than a couple of acres, but the man who was selling it said I had to take all or nothing. He didn't want the headache and I loved the view so we came to a reasonable agreement." Devon squeezed Elaine's hand. "I had this area developed because I didn't want to touch that field of wildflowers. The land where the house is now had almost no growth, so it just seemed perfect."

Devon pointed just beyond the trees. "A few years ago people began moving in down the road and the county finally paved the road all the way down to my house. I thought I would mind having asphalt to my door, but the truth is that I really don't miss the washboard ruts at all."

Elaine looked back out over the property. "Just how much of this land is yours?"

Devon thought about it for a moment. "Um, let's see… from the edge of the fence over there, I guess it goes about a mile back up toward the neighbor's house." She turned her attention to the other side of the house. "It extends out that way probably a couple of miles or more. It butts up next to Bureau of Land Management land so I know that no one will be building on that side of me."

Elaine pointed out toward the back of the property. "How about that direction?"

Devon bit her lip while she mentally measured. "Oh three or four miles, I guess."

Elaine laughed. "You don't know how many acres you own?"

Devon shrugged. "I don't really feel like I own the land. I'm just kind of borrowing it."

Elaine blinked. "It must have been some deal."

"What?" Devon had been chewing on her lip, worried that Elaine would get the wrong idea about her. She made a good living and she had a nice sum of money saved, but she would definitely not be considered wealthy by most people's standards.

Elaine raised an eyebrow. "The deal that you made with the man who sold all this to you. It must have been a hell of a deal."

"Turned out that way. He ran the local nursery. After all, I was a good customer. I bought plants, killed them and bought more." She sipped her coffee. "He'd inherited all of this, didn't have family and wanted to make sure someone would go on limiting development out here. Eventually, I'd like to grant some of it to the BLM. There's just not enough green space in this world."

"It suits you."

Does it suit you, Devon wanted to ask her. Could Elaine picture herself living here too? The question trembled on her lips, but it was just too soon. No need for a U-Haul. Elaine had some baggage named Grace that still troubled her.

Not sure what to say, she did the one thing that always seemed right—she slipped into Elaine's arms and kissed her.

No longer surprised by her carnal thoughts when Devon was around, Elaine held her tight and considered what it would be like to make love to her on the deck with nothing but stars to cover them. Everything else about Devon's house suited her personality as well. It was nice without being overbearing. It fit perfectly into the landscape. The furniture was softly worn and comfortable, inviting any visitor to stay. There was absolutely no pretense here.

The phone rang, startling them apart. Devon returned with the receiver cradled against her ear.

"Raine, what do you mean, I sound different?" She winked at Elaine.

Devon paused to listen again and started laughing. Her breath caught as Devon looked at her with a smoldering gaze. "I sound tired? You are the one about to deliver any day now. Yes, it was a tiring assignment, but I slept good last night." Devon flashed a wink at her.

Devon continued to laugh before finally saying, "Okay. Okay. Yes, Raine, I'll be over to see you later today just like I said. Okay. I love you too. Bye." Devon hung up the phone and placed it on the rail before stepping back into Elaine's arms.

"What time do you have to go to work?" she asked. She wasn't looking forward to the prospect of Devon leaving, but she had to be realistic. As much as she may want to, they couldn't hide away forever.

"I have to run the samples I collected by the lab, which shouldn't take long. Then I thought we could stop by Raine's for a little while, if you don't mind." Devon was studying her for a reaction.

Elated and scared all at once, she asked, "You aren't going to tell Raine that you are bringing company with you?"

Devon laughed and wrapped her arms around Elaine. "Are

you kidding? First, she wouldn't let me off the phone because she would be peppering me with questions. Second, I didn't want her to drop my nephew right there on the kitchen floor."

Elaine laughed. "I would love to meet your sister, sweetheart."

"Maybe after we go to Raine's and the lab we could stop off for an early dinner…hmm?"

Elaine loved her teasing tone. "Dinner?"

Devon cocked her head to the side as she smiled at Elaine. "I do need to keep your strength up after all."

"And why is that Dr. McKinney?"

"Because, Captain Thomas, I fully intend to bring you back here and wear you out all over again." Devon could feel the shiver that passed through Elaine's body and delighted in her response.

"Mmm, I like the sound of that," Elaine murmured against Devon's lips before capturing her mouth in a probing kiss.

Elaine knew where the EPA office was. When they arrived Elaine was pleased with Devon's invitation to come into her office with her. She had thought that she would wait in the truck while Devon ran in.

Still Elaine teased, "You only want me to come in so I can help you carry these boxes."

Devon flashed her a smile. "Hey, I'm no fool."

A woman left her microscope to relieve Devon of the box she was carrying. She plopped the box on the near table and greeted Devon with a warm hug. "Hey Dev, it's good to have you back."

Devon smiled at her. "You may not think so when you see what I brought for you."

Elaine gingerly set down the box she was carrying next to Devon's, then dusted her hands. Devon performed introductions.

"Captain Elaine Thomas of the US Forest Service this is Dr. Ginger Grant of the EPA."

They exchanged pleasantries as a larger man emerged from

an office. He too greeted Elaine. An easy smile lit up his face. "Evan Morris."

Before Elaine could respond, he had directed his attention to Devon. "I read your daily field reports, but look forward to the comprehensive analysis. I'll have Carl start getting these samples into the scanning electron microscope right away so we can see what we really have. How'd things look up there?"

"Starting to return slowly but surely. Maybe in a few more years we'll see some real changes."

They quickly dropped into work jargon, allowing Elaine to watch the way Devon interacted with her colleagues. There was a lot of respect between them, it showed, but they all also had matching frowns of concern as they gestured at their work stations and files. Like many government staffers, they had so much to do and not enough time to do it.

The talked turned personal, so there was affection there as well. Devon patiently answered the onslaught of rapidly fired questions about being out in the cold, the snowstorm, Raine, the baby, Phillip and Stacey.

Elaine was aware of a few curious glances directed at her—why was she still hanging out with Devon? She tried not to blush or fidget. In another setting she'd probably get the third degree. Evan's manner was distinctly paternal.

After a few more minutes they finally managed to break free from the gathering and took their leave.

Once in the truck Devon reached over and held Elaine's hand. Raine didn't live but maybe five minutes from the lab, in a nice suburb. Elaine took it all in, feeling slightly overwhelmed. She was silently processing the details of Devon's life when they pulled into the driveway of a well-kept one-story brick home.

Before Devon could even knock the door swung open and a very pregnant woman threw herself into Devon's embrace. Elaine stood to the side, smiling, as the two women talked simultaneously, but amazingly seemed to keep up with the other's conversation.

Finally, Raine stepped back and ushered them in. Her astute eyes didn't miss the fact that Devon reached for Elaine's hand as they walked in.

"What would you two like to drink?"

"Raine, sit down and I'll get it."

"Don't 'Raine' me, Devon. Sit down and let me treat you like the guests in my home that you are. I've had about enough of Stacey not letting me do a thing for myself." Raine turned and began venting her obvious frustration with Stacey's over-the-top protectiveness.

"I mean look at me. The doctor said putting on some weight is healthy, but Stacey is here three times a day making sure I'm the size of a cow."

Devon couldn't help but laugh and then laugh harder as her sister scowled. She reluctantly acquiesced and joined Elaine on the sofa.

"So what would you like to drink? Iced tea, soda, water?"

Devon looked at Elaine for her preference and then back to Raine. "Tea sounds great."

A moment later, Raine returned with two glasses of tea and Elaine almost burst out laughing when she saw the mint sprig in the top of her glass. *It must run in the family.*

When Raine went back to the kitchen to get her own beverage Devon smiled and pulled the mint leaf from Elaine's glass. She licked it, stroked it with her tongue and sucked on it before she finally placed it in her mouth.

Elaine was excruciatingly wet. "You did that on purpose," she accused.

"So?" She turned to give her sister an angelic smile.

Elaine was increasingly aware of Raine's scrutiny as the sisters talked. The two were a lot alike in that they were both very perceptive. But it wasn't exactly like Devon was doing a damn thing to try and hide the nature of their relationship.

Raine broke off mid-sentence and grabbed her side. Devon nearly leapt across the coffee table to put her hand on Raine's stomach.

Raine gave her a sideways glare. "Oh, I see. No 'Raine are you okay? Raine can I get you anything?' You just want to feel the baby kick. While you find that amazing and wonderful and sweet, I'll have you know that's my rib he's breaking."

"You love it and you know it."

Raine ignored her sister and turned her attention to Elaine. "I swear I used to think lesbians had the right idea. Now I think you're all just nuts. Stacey just wants to play Godmother, Devon can't wait to be Auntie Dev and Phillip...well, Phillip is so in for it when he gets home. He's here long enough to get me pregnant and enjoy himself and then leaves me to push something roughly the size of a football out of my body. It isn't natural I tell you!"

After a moment Devon moved back to the sofa, tucking her legs underneath her and leaning into Elaine. Raine pointed at them but addressed her sister. "So, tell me about this. You didn't say anything on the phone."

Devon smiled up at Elaine and then back at her sister. "Elaine is a captain with the US Forest Service," Devon paused to wink at Elaine, "and my babysitter while I was up there."

Raine smiled at Elaine. "And you thought she might need some more babysitting when she returned home?"

Elaine threw her head back in amusement. "Yeah, something like that."

Devon rolled her eyes. "Yes, Raine, Elaine is my lover. Are you happy now?"

Raine beamed. "If it wasn't so much work to get out of this chair I would come over there and give you a hug. It's about damn time Dev met someone." Raine paused and tapped the fingertips of each hand together. "Now if we could just get the elusive Ms. Stacey Bailey to settle down."

"As a matter of fact it would seem our very own Stacey has met a woman who she *actually* wants to see again, but this mysterious woman wants nothing to do with her."

Raine almost squealed in delight. "I know that you are going to pay for giving me this information, Dev and for that I'm sorry, but thank you, thank you, thank you. This I can use." Raine's eyes took on a mischievous gleam. "And yes, I know Stacey has only been mothering me because she loves me. But she has been worse than I think Mom would be and if tormenting her with this is all the satisfaction I get then bless you!"

Devon laughed and the two sisters continued to talk, including Elaine in the conversation the entire time. Devon took all three of their empty glasses to the kitchen where she rinsed them and set them in the dishwasher. She helped her sister to her feet for a hug.

"Elaine and I are going to slip out for dinner." Devon winked at her sister. "Besides I'm not going to be around when Stacey gets here with your dinner and finds out that you met Elaine first."

Raine laughed and walked them to the door. "Elaine, it was nice to meet you." This time Raine did hug Elaine, to the extent her stomach would allow. "I'll see you two soon."

Devon smiled. "Yes, you will."

Chapter 18

"I've never been the way I am with you. It's like I can't get enough of you. I have this urgent need for you all the time," Elaine whispered the following morning.

Devon kissed her forehead gently and ran her finger across Elaine's lips. "Baby, I feel the same way."

Baby. God, she loved the sound of that rolling off Devon's lips.

She rested her chin on the arm that draped over Devon. "You drive me crazy; you know that, don't you?"

Devon lazily rubbed her back, a smile tugged at her lips. "I hope you mean that in a good way."

Her smile was slow and lazy. "I mean that in the very best way."

Devon leaned up and kissed her. "It's only right that I should drive you crazy after the way you ravaged me last night."

"I absolutely did not ravage you!" she stated with mock indignation.

Devon continued to laugh. "If you say so."

"I got a little...aggressive. I can't help it if I lose control with you. How is that my fault?"

"Elaine, you are an amazing and responsive lover. I absolutely love the way you show me what you want and when you want it."

Sudden banging on the front door had them both stumbling out of bed.

"Get out of bed," someone yelled.

Her heart was pounding in alarm, but Devon's mirth was palpable as she struggled into her robe. She'd scarcely opened the door when she was promptly swept into the visitor's arms. "Welcome back, love."

For the briefest of moments she felt a pang of jealousy like none she had ever felt before and then she recognized Stacey from her picture. She hoped the jeans and Tee she'd pulled on were tidy enough.

"I couldn't wait another day to see you. I get a phone call two days ago and then nothing."

Devon laughed and hugged her again. "I've been a little busy."

Stacey met Elaine's gaze over Devon's shoulder. One eyebrow lifted.

Devon stepped away from Stacey and Elaine felt a strange sense of relief when she saw Devon's expression. The look that told her that Devon was right where she wanted to be when she stepped into the circle of Elaine's arms. Once Elaine had recognized Stacey all feelings of jealousy were gone. Devon had said that they were best friends, almost like sisters and Elaine trusted that.

"Stacey, this is Elaine. Elaine, I would like you to meet Stacey."

Again the soft accent flowed as Stacey took her hand in a firm grip. "It's very nice to meet you, Elaine."

Stacey looked at Devon. Apparently, Devon read something in her eyes that Elaine wasn't able to decode. It was as if the two were telepathic and words weren't needed to convey their thoughts.

"It's nice to finally meet you, too."

Devon arched a questioning eyebrow at Stacey but said nothing. Apparently this was a silent exchange that held some sort of significance.

Stacey opted for a chair across from the sofa where Devon settled into Elaine's embrace. Even when they were alone and just sitting together this had quickly become their most comfortable position and Elaine loved it.

Stacey arched a brow, a knowing smile tugging at her lips. "I take it you had a good trip then?"

"Yes, I was able to complete my work despite some snow."

"I was worried about you. It was damn cold here. I can't imagine how bad it was up there." Stacey looked directly at Elaine and smiled. "Good thing she found someone to keep her warm, eh?"

Elaine couldn't help but grin at Stacey's innuendo. "Something like that."

"How long have you been a ranger?"

"About fourteen years."

"You must really enjoy your job."

"Yes, I do. I knew early on what I wanted to do. So when I went to college, my decision was already made. So I just jumped right in." She found herself saying more than she planned, but this was Devon's best friend—if the conversation was a test, life would be so much easier if she passed.

Stacey nodded in understanding. "Devon was exactly the same way. There aren't too many teenagers who long to become botanists, but as soon as Devon learned that there were people who studied plants for a living, that was all she wanted to do. There was no stopping her."

Elaine enjoyed hearing about Devon from someone else's perspective and wasn't overly happy when she glanced at the clock and realized that she needed to get ready for work.

Devon must have noticed the same thing because she turned

to Elaine, "You're going to be late for work if you don't get showered and on your way."

"I know. I have to drop stuff at the house first. Duty calls. If you'll excuse me. Stacey, it was really nice to meet you."

"Likewise."

As Elaine made her way down the hall to take a shower, she heard Stacey leave.

Elaine heard the shower door and sensed Devon behind her. "We can't have that kind of shower."

"I know. I love being with you, though."

Hair barely dry, Devon walked Elaine to her truck. "Do you want to have dinner out tonight? Or perhaps go visit Raine? I haven't been very good at keeping you out of bed."

Their kiss was gentle and sweet and left Elaine wanting more. "You haven't heard me complaining have you?"

Devon smiled. "What time will you be home?"

Devon's question created a wave in Elaine's stomach. *Home.*

"It might be later than usual. I need to stop by my house and get a change of clothes and unload some stuff. But I'll call you when I'm on my way. We can do whatever you like tonight. As long as I'm with you, that's all that matters." Elaine rested her forehead against Devon's.

"You could leave some changes of clothes here so that you don't have to do this every day, unless, of course, you want to."

The truth was that there was nothing but "stuff" at her house. She needed to water her plants weekly, but that was about it. Reminders of Grace would be everywhere. The thought of going to what used to be their home just made her tired.

But the thought of bringing more of her clothes to Devon's house was unnerving. Everything about it felt right. But that was how it had started with Grace as well. Elaine mentally scolded herself. The two were nothing alike.

"I'll do that," was all she said, but it felt momentous.

Devon laughed again and pulled Elaine's head down for a deep kiss.

"You better get going. Be careful, babe. See you tonight."

Elaine drove quickly to the house she had shared with Grace. She ignored the lingering signs, the few items that Grace hadn't taken with her, tossed her gear and bags into the bedroom and headed for the station.

On the drive, Elaine couldn't help but think about what was awaiting her. She had loved her time off with Devon, not to mention their time in the mountains, but now it was time to return to her regular duties and people at the station. Oddly enough, she was filled with both excitement and dread. She had missed her crew and outside of Donovan, hadn't seen any of them in over a month. On the other hand, there was Grace. There was little doubt she would run into her at some point and she wasn't looking forward to it. But things had changed—she might dread it, but she wasn't afraid of it or cowed by the past. Nevertheless, she wouldn't mind if it was some time before their paths crossed.

Chapter 19

Devon was first to rise and gently slipped from under Elaine's arm toward the shower. As she lathered her body, she thought about Elaine. It was hard to believe it had already been two weeks since they returned from the mountains, every night of which Elaine had stayed at her house. The past week had been hard. Elaine had worked several late nights and by the time she went by her house and then made it to Devon's, it was even later, allowing them not nearly enough time together.

She heard the bathroom door open and hoped she hadn't made too much noise and disturbed Elaine's sleep. She had looked so peaceful and Devon wanted to let her get as much rest as possible.

"Good morning, beautiful," Devon heard just over the water spray.

"Good morning. Did I wake you?"

"No. I had to get up. I need to get to the station early today.

Leave the water on."

After Devon exited the shower she planted a soft kiss on her lover's lips before retreating to the bedroom while Elaine took her position in the shower. Just minutes later as she watched Elaine retrieve her uniform from her bag and shake it vigorously in an attempt to get some of the wrinkles out, she decided that enough was enough.

She motioned toward the bag. "Okay, this is just ridiculous."

"What is?"

Devon arched an eyebrow. "You bringing a bag over every night."

Elaine felt her stomach drop. "But…"

Before Elaine could say more, the phone rang, startling them both. It was unusually early to be getting a phone call and Devon ran to the phone.

She was surprised to hear the frantic tone in Stacey's voice. "Raine's water just broke and we're on our way to the hospital."

Immediately, Devon gathered her coat and keys. "I'll meet you there." She hung up the phone. Turning she found Elaine standing directly behind her, concern etched on her face.

"Raine is in labor. Her water just broke and she and Stacey are on their way to the hospital."

"Okay. Just breathe. Do you want me to drop you off?"

"No. I know you have important things to take care of at work."

"Are you sure?"

Devon slipped into Elaine's arms. "Yes, I'm sure. Go handle your business so you can join us as soon as you're finished."

"All right, I'll be there as soon as I can."

"We'll be at Mercy Hospital on Fourth and Oxford. I'll let you know the room number as soon as I find out." With a quick peck on the lips, Devon was out the door.

"Be careful," Elaine called to her as she ran out the door.

She latched her seat belt and wondered if she'd imagined that Elaine looked a bit…hurt. Silly thought. On her cell phone, she called Evan to let him know that Raine was in labor and she probably wouldn't be back for several days. Evan had been waiting for this news and told her to call and let him know that Raine was okay.

Devon was once again grateful for the relationships she had built with her co-workers. Everyone respected her and her work and no one begrudged her the time she spent out of the office. Raine and Stacey had been in several times and everyone treated them as though they too were family. They had even started a betting pool on when Raine would have her baby. Most of them had come to Raine's baby shower or sent gifts. Devon couldn't have chosen a better group of people to work with.

Devon knew that Raine was in good hands with Stacey, but she had promised Raine that she would be there with her and she meant to keep that promise. She ran into the hospital and after demanding the information was immediately directed to Raine's room. She walked in to find Raine calmly reading a magazine while Stacey was pacing.

"Hey, how are you doing?"

"Dev, I'm glad you are here."

Before anyone could speak, Raine's doctor sauntered into the birthing room. Like Raine, he looked unhurried and unalarmed. After a quick check he announced, "It's going to be a while yet. Your contractions are still relatively far apart. It might be awhile before he's ready to greet us. I'll be back in a little bit to see where we are. Until then, the nurses will be checking you and if you need anything just push the call button."

"Thank you, Dr. Archer." Raine spoke calmly as she turned her attention to Stacey, "See, nothing to worry about. I told you that you didn't have to drive like a crazy person to get me here. Now will you have a seat, please? Your pacing is making me dizzy." The relief that washed over Stacey was almost comical.

Devon pulled out her cell phone and sent Elaine a brief text message updating her on Raine's condition and giving her the room number.

"Elaine had to check in at work before coming to the hospital. I expect her to call or show up soon." She checked her watch as Raine flipped the page of her magazine.

A few moments later, a nurse entered the room. "Time to walk."

All three of them looked at her inquisitively. "Walk where?" Stacey asked, looking a bit pale.

"We are going to try to speed this up. Just walk up and down the halls a few times and then rest. Do your best to walk the same course every thirty minutes."

"Okay, Raine, you heard the woman. Let's go for a little walk." Devon did her best to sound calm, even though inside she felt as nervous as Stacey looked.

Raine had one hand on Devon's arm as they paced the corridors. Devon was surprised when Raine asked, "So is Elaine the one?"

"The one?"

Raine quietly laughed. "Dev, you've been glowing since you came back from your trip. When I saw you with Elaine you were, I don't know…different."

"How so?"

Raine was quiet for a moment. "I don't know. I mean…you seem so comfortable with Elaine…so happy."

"I know I am in love with her. I hope she wants to be the one."

Raine stopped walking and appraised her sister. "Dev, you're a little slow if you don't know the answer to that question by now. All anyone has to do is look at the two of you together to see that the woman is absolutely smitten with you."

Devon gave her sister a hug. "I hope you're right. I was about to ask her to move in when Stacey called."

"About to, huh? So when *are* you going to ask her?"

"Well, in case you haven't noticed, I have my hands full with a pregnant woman…literally."

"Excuses, excuses," Raine mocked playfully. She lowered her

voice. "Since we are out of the room and away from Stacey can you please explain to her I'm about to be a mother and don't need to be coddled any longer?"

Devon smiled again and tears welled in her eyes. "Yes. And you are going to be a mother, aren't you?"

She'd had nine months to adjust to a pregnant Raine, but now that the time had finally arrived, the reality began to sink in.

"Yes. I am."

Devon looked proudly at her sister. "When did you get all grown up?"

Raine rolled her eyes. "Oh, I don't know. Maybe when I got married. Started having sex. Got pregnant. Decided to have a husband who the government called up at the most inconvenient time to play soldier boy... And oh yeah! My sister left me with a *mad* woman!"

Devon couldn't help but laugh, especially when Stacey stuck her head out of the doorway and frowned at them both.

Raine simply pointed. "See what I mean."

Devon nodded in agreement. "Just imagine how protective of this little guy she'll be?"

"She better be ten times worse with him." Raine's voice caught as a contraction washed over her.

Stacey gripped the hospital safety rail looking as though she might faint. Devon could have sworn she heard Stacey mutter something about "what was she thinking letting Raine get pregnant" but she was too focused on her sister to catch much of what Stacey was saying.

"If you pass out you're on your own. I'm busy here." Devon flicked a brief glance in Stacey's direction.

Once Raine was resettled, a no-nonsense labor nurse carrying ice chips and a cool wet cloth entered. She took Raine's vitals and chased Stacey and Devon out of the room while she checked Raine's progress.

Amused that the always unflappable Stacey was anything but poised, Devon took pity on her. "Why don't you focus on getting the video for Phillip set up?"

Stacey visibly steadied. "I'll go get my camera and gear from the car."

Ten hours later, Raine was screaming for drugs as her contractions increased in both frequency and duration.

"The nurse said the doctor will be here in a few minutes," Devon announced anxiously.

"Thank God." Stacey mumbled, looking both exhausted and excited.

Elaine, having briefly observed the scene from the doorway, patted Raine on the leg as she dropped a quick kiss on Devon's cheek. Her sweetheart looked anxious and she didn't want to get in the way. She hoped she was welcome, but after Devon's statement that her staying every night was ridiculous, she wasn't so sure. "Hang in there, Raine. I'll just wait outside and give you some privacy."

"You'll do no such thing. Get your ass back in here," Raine commanded breathlessly. "I was hoping you wouldn't mind holding the video camera and filming because I think Stace is going to pass out."

Stacey's protest was weak enough that Elaine thought Raine might be right. She could barely control the breaking of her voice "Sure. It would be my pleasure."

The doctor entered followed by two nurses and began final preparations for the baby's impending arrival. Stacey maneuvered herself behind Raine, holding her up and making it easier for her to push. Elaine managed the video camera while Devon stood over her sister, gently stroking her forehead.

"Just a couple more," the doctor urged in his steady, confident voice.

Stacey encouraged Raine as she maintained a death grip on Stacey's arm. Raine was sweating and crying as the baby's head finally began to crown. One final push and the next thing Devon knew the doctor was cutting the umbilical cord.

"A perfect baby boy," the doctor stated. It seemed to take forever for the doctor and nurses to administer the baby's Apgar score and clean him up. But just minutes later the nurse was laying Raine's perfectly healthy, tightly wrapped son in her arms.

It took Devon a moment to feel the tears that were streaming down her cheeks. Raine was radiant and her son was perfect. He was red and wrinkly and had Phillip's eyes and Raine's mouth. He had ten fingers, ten toes and he was definitely a McKinney. When he opened his mouth and yawned, Raine looked at Devon, Elaine and Stacey and they all laughed.

"As if he did all the work," Raine said, her voice strained with fatigue. He wrapped his little hand around Raine's pinky and looked up at the women looking lovingly down on him.

Stacey said, "Let's get the video chat going."

Raine didn't take her gaze off her son. "Little man, you're gonna meet your papa."

Elaine set the video camera in the tripod making sure it was perfectly positioned on Raine and the baby while Stacey worked some kind of magic on her laptop. There was some delay while Phillip made his way to the space on his base where he could see and respond.

Once his beaming, anxious face came onto the screen on Stacey's laptop, Devon said, "Let's leave them alone. Hard enough he's on the other side of the world."

"He's so beautiful honey," Devon heard her say into the camera. "He's perfect. I wish you could have been here."

Phillip might not be here now, but Devon was glad that he would be able to share in the experience later.

Stacey went to find a beverage and Devon knew she needed a few minutes to collect herself. Stacey absolutely hated getting weepy in front of anyone except maybe Devon.

Elaine and Devon made their way down the elevator and to the small garden outside the visitor's lounge. Devon immediately took shelter in Elaine's arms, shedding tears of joy while Elaine simply held her without saying anything.

Just a few moments later Devon wiped her eyes. "I'm sorry."

"For what?"

"For crying and getting you all wet." She tried to lighten her mood. "God, I must look terrible."

Elaine placed her finger under Devon's chin and tilted her head up, pushing a stray hair behind her ear. "You are by far the most incredible woman I have ever seen in my life and please don't ever apologize for showing your emotions."

Elaine leaned down to kiss her. The kiss was gentle and sweet and asked nothing of her.

Once she had calmed they made their way back to Raine's room. The video chat session was just ending. She could hear good-natured ribbing and congratulations being offered as the connection closed.

"He's beautiful, Raine. You and Phillip made a perfect baby."

"We agreed on his name for certain," Raine said. "Adam Paul, this is your Aunt Devon."

Devon didn't even hide the emotion in her voice as Raine introduced the child named after their father. "Hello Adam. Welcome to the world." Devon bent down and kissed her sister on the forehead. "I love you."

Raine's eyes glittered with tears as she looked at her sister. Her whisper was filled with emotion. "I love you too, Dev."

They all stood around Raine adoring her son until the nurse finally chased them out so mother and son could rest. Devon and Stacey both dropped a kiss on Raine's head and gave her a hug.

Devon gave Stacey a hug in the parking lot and realized she was still shaking.

"I'm so glad it's over," Stacey said after clearing her throat. "That was amazing and freaky and exhausting, all at once."

"Are you hungry? We could get some breakfast," Elaine suggested.

"Breakfast? Okay, then after I want to sleep." Devon gazed at the hint of sunrise. It was a brand-new day.

Chapter 20

"Shower, then sleep," Devon announced as they arrived home.

"What a good idea." Elaine wanted a hot shower desperately and knew it would help to soothe and relax them both.

She joined Devon in the shower and gently washed her, at that moment wanting nothing more than to take care of her. She slowly dried Devon, concerned by the dark circles around her eyes. She looked like she would fall over at any minute. Elaine had spent days awake during fire season. When the adrenaline stopped pumping, she knew how the exhaustion would sap any strength that may have been left.

Moments later she crawled in bed next to Devon and pulled her into her arms. She thought Devon would fall asleep as soon as her head hit the pillow, but instead Devon's hands began slowly rubbing over Elaine's shoulders and stomach. She couldn't stifle the gasp of pleasure when Devon took an erect nipple between her teeth.

She knew she should insist that Devon rest. She wasn't a selfish lover. But as always with Devon, it only took a touch and her body was on fire. Devon kissed her slowly, deeply as their bodies began to merge. Devon's hands slid lower pulling Elaine's hips beneath her as her tongue swept across her lips.

She pulled Devon close against her. "I intended to just hold you while you slept."

Devon quietly said, "I need you."

She leaned up to kiss Devon and all at once the urgency was there. As she slowly stroked Devon's body she could feel her yielding, her body silently begging Elaine to take her. Devon's body was so soft, warm and inviting. The low moans encouraged her to continue. All of those weeks ago in the mountains Elaine felt like she had shed her old life. Now, in Devon's arms, she felt like she was reborn.

Elaine was lost in sleep, slowly awaking from her dreams of erotic memories of their lovemaking. The sound of someone talking in the distance caused her to stir. The bed was much too soft and her body too relaxed for her to be at work. The voice at the edge of her sleep was brief and soft and then the room was quiet again as she drifted back into a deep sleep.

When Elaine finally awoke she had no idea what time it was. The room was still dark and she listened a moment before she realized that the steady patter of rain was trying to lull her back to sleep again. She felt Devon move against her and she knew that if there truly was a heaven she had found it. It was right here in this moment, in this bed, with this woman.

"Are you awake?"

"Don't want to be," she answered. "But we need to go back to the hospital. Raine will be discharged today."

Now or never, she thought. Retreating to silence wouldn't get her anywhere. "When you said that my coming over every night was ridiculous—"

"What?" Devon sat up. "I never said that."

"You pointed at my bag and said it was ridiculous. I've been here every night since we got back. I assumed you meant that it was too much."

"No, that is not what I meant...at all."

Elaine wiped sleep out of her eyes. "Okay. So, what did you mean?"

"I meant that it is ridiculous for you to have to stop by your house every day. It is ridiculous because I asked you to bring more of your things over and yet you still live out of that bag. It is ridiculous because I am completely and totally in love with you and I want you and *all* your things here *all* the time." Devon's eyes were shining in the low light.

Elaine trembled as she listened to the words she herself had been feeling. "You do know that I'm hopelessly and helplessly in love with you."

She leaned down and gently kissed Elaine. "Well?"

"Yes."

Chapter 21

The fire in northern Oregon was burning out of control. The winter snow for the area hadn't been enough to dent the decade-long drought conditions that had intensified as summer arrived. High winds and a lack of rain were propelling the blaze. An endless stream of beetle-killed trees were in the path of the fire. The environmentalists hadn't wanted the trees clear-cut and now they presented a hazard to the hundreds of firefighters risking their lives trying to battle the inferno as it consumed thousands of acres and numerous homes.

Elaine made what she hoped was one of the last pit stops at her house before heading to the station. She intended to put it on the market, but the last few months had flown by. All she wanted to do every day was get home to Devon.

It was already early afternoon. They would carpool to the staging area where they would await orders from incident command for mobilization. From there they were sure to work through the night. Her crew was well-trained and would probably be among the frontline firefighters working to create fire breaks. For the first time she thought about how dangerous this part of her job was. She had a family to go home to. She smiled at the sensation that thought brought. For the first time since her relationship with her parents had become estranged, she was part of something so much bigger than herself and it had nothing to do with work.

"There were multiple start points, all at once—if this isn't arson I'll eat my hat," Donovan said as he tossed his gear into the back of Elaine's truck.

If Elaine thought too long about it, she'd be too angry to think. "The National Guard is doing what it can with the aerial assaults. Preliminary reports have us working with other ground crews to create breaks on the northern perimeter."

Donovan wore a mischievous smirk. "Let's hope they don't drop any of that shit on us this time." His smirk became a full-on grin. "I thought you'd be a redhead for months."

Elaine laughed. She remembered that incident well. They had called for a foam drop and the ferric oxide had coated them all in red. It had taken her weeks to get all of the residue out of her hair. Thankfully satellite imaging and GPS coordination had improved so much in the last few years that those sorts of mishaps were less likely. "Laugh it up. If memory serves, you complained about itching for days. Besides you looked so cute all pink!"

Donovan shot her a good-natured frown. "Yeah, it stung a little too."

She saw Donovan tuck a photo of his wife into his pocket, a standard talisman. Something she'd never felt quite right doing with a picture of Grace. Now she was kicking herself for not having a photo of Devon for herself. She ached to go back for another kiss and gave herself a hard mental shake. If she was going to do her job and get her crew and herself through this alive she was going to have to stay focused. She was going to have to push Devon from her mind. *Yeah right!*

At Incident Command, outside of The Dalles, their crew joined hundreds of other personnel from federal departments, queuing up for buses to their work sites. She pushed thoughts of Devon to the back of her mind. She was a ranger, a captain. She had a job to do and people to lead and protect.

Elaine reported to the command post and received orders to head toward the northeast ridge. The commander pointed out two specific points on the topographical map.

"The wind is expected to shift and we need that break or the fire goes up this entire ridge. We have bulldozers in the leading path of the fire. Hopefully we can contain it on the eastern edge."

"Yes, sir," Elaine answered. If the wind did shift as expected they would have precious little time to get a break established before the approach of the fire. Ultimately, they would be in the direct path of the blaze. Her crew was going to have to work quickly while the planes and helicopters provided what support they could. The high winds made it dangerous to fly so air support would be limited, but the water trucks would be extremely useful on the ground.

Most of the men and women that Elaine worked with had families, all of whom she had made promises to—promises that their loved ones would return home safely. She knew that it was not a promise she should make, but it was a promise that she intended to keep.

The crew would be riding in on a water truck armed with shovels, axes and chainsaws as they headed into the night. The truck dropped them at the end of a fire road close to where they would begin clearing vegetation. If they were lucky there would be some natural breaks that would help ease their burden. The tanker truck would follow them as they created the firebreak and the crew of the truck would work to soak as much area as they could before having to rotate out with another truck to resupply their stores.

It was twilight as they approached the ridge, the smoke was

191

almost suffocating. The kerchiefs they wore weren't really much help and the smoke burned their lungs. If the blaze did shift they would have to switch to oxygen tanks, but for now they would conserve their resources.

The burn in Elaine's body was familiar and she worked through the heaviness that was pervading her muscles. With chainsaws and shovels they worked to cut trees and remove anything that would fuel the blaze. They had been working for several hours without rest and had managed to clear a wide path. She guessed it was after midnight, though the eerie light from the approaching fire made the light uncertain. The tanker crew stayed with them spraying water on the surrounding area hoping to saturate it, leaving the fire nothing to feed on.

"Allen, get some water on those trees." The smoke burned Elaine's throat, making it difficult to yell. The roar of the fire nearly swallowed her words.

"Yes, Cap." His voice was showing the effects of the smoke as well.

The wind kicked up again and, as predicted, turned in their direction. Embers leapt and jumped, starting smaller fires they quickly used their shovels to smother with dirt.

"Okay guys, watch your back!"

For a moment it looked like the break would hold. But as they worked she felt the smoke getting heavier. The fire was gaining in intensity.

"Come on guys, pick up the pace. Watch the crosswinds."

"Cap, you got a hot spot to your left."

Elaine quickly smothered the fire. "Thanks, Dex!"

Her focus abruptly riveted on the radio chatter. A team farther up the ridge was pulling back. The fire had crossed over them and was coming up behind Elaine's crew even as the other team was in the back burn with a second wave of fire rising.

Their clear-cut had been breached and the entire company was encircled. It was a call nobody ever wanted to hear and she knew that her crew was the closest ground unit to assist the trapped firefighters.

Elaine had the safety of her crew to think about but when it came right down to it, the decision she had to make was easy. She redirected the water truck that was working with them and still over half full, to lay down a clearing to give the trapped firefighters a path out of danger.

"Those guys are going to need some help getting out of there. We are going to break off this spur and go assist," she yelled. "But anyone who wants out now should go. You have families to think about."

"So do you, Cap."

Elaine smiled; it was ironic that those words had never been spoken when she was with Grace.

Elaine looked into the faces of the men and women standing around her waiting for orders. None had even budged, not that she had expected them to. They all knew that if they were in the same situation they would want help to come as quickly as possible. Their eyes held fear but also loyalty and a determination to do whatever was necessary to save lives.

A helicopter had been dispatched to assist the stranded firefighters, but there was no guarantee that it would be enough. Within minutes, she knew the water drop wouldn't be enough. They all knew it—she saw it in the faces of her crew.

The fire was burning too hot for the water to extinguish much of a path. The secondary plane's payload of chemical retardant still wasn't guaranteed to alleviate the immediate danger. Elaine checked the coordinates and the direction of the wind. The fire was moving faster than the rangers would be able to. They were about to be just as pinned down as the crew they'd come to rescue.

They were trapped with a granite ridge they couldn't climb to their west and encroaching fire on the south and east, both converging on the fresh fuel, drawing the fire right over them to the north.

Their only escape route was going to be ablaze before they cleared it.

She radioed the captain of the trapped crew. He had reached the same conclusion and agreed to work their way toward her crew where they would work to establish a back door for extraction.

The air drop was directed to the leading edge of the fire separating Elaine's crew from the trapped men. Hopefully it would provide them with more time and room to work.

When her company arrived at the fire wall that separated her from the trapped unit, the water truck was already working. They were in oxygen tanks and Elaine's own men quickly donned theirs. They began moving burning and smoldering material out of the way.

The smoke made it impossible to breathe and despite the flames they had almost no visibility. They were close to the water drop site, had to be, because now steam was making an ash slick of the helmet's visor. The fire surrounded them but the small area they had cleared to reach the trapped men and women was holding.

They were on top of the other crew before she realized it. Amid gestured high fives they turned to their mutual path of escape, the crews joined forces to clear a path. Elaine tried to see through the blackness of the smoke. She did a quick head count—and came up one short. Someone was missing. Driven by instinct alone, she turned and ran back into the fire.

She almost tripped over the missing man. She thought it might be Donovan, but the number and visor was too obscured to be sure. It didn't matter, he was down and she wasn't leaving without him.

Despite the protective clothing she wore she could feel the blisters forming on her skin. They had very little time before they would become victims of the fire. If hell did exist, she had no doubt that she was standing in the midst of it.

Wrapping her arms around the fallen man's chest just under his arms, she began backing out the way she had come in. Her legs burned as she dug her boots into the smoldering earth.

She didn't have to turn to feel the heat build at her back. There was no doubt in her mind that her men would hold the door open. She felt like the blood was about to boil in her veins, when Dex and Allen appeared to take her burden from her. Through sheer will and determination, she remained on her feet. Their goal now was to hold the clearing they had created open a little while longer.

Where the fuck is that second plane?

The trapped crew had suffered significant burns and smoke inhalation. The oxygen helped but they needed to get medical attention. She knew she had some minor burns and the rest of her crew needed help. They didn't have hours. They might not even have minutes—

The honking of horns penetrated the roar of the fire. Two trucks were a welcome sight as they picked their way across the uneven terrain toward them. The smoke was so thick Elaine couldn't be certain of how they had made it in to them. The drivers had hoped to carry one crew out but there were now too many. Elaine ordered the most severely injured and exhausted to the trucks. The rest of them would have to hike out as quickly as possible.

She looked back at the main fire and ordered immediate mobilization. With their heavy gear and no rock climbing equipment, they could only follow the routes the trucks had taken, at a fraction of their speed. If they could make it to the break they had worked on clearing earlier they would have a better chance of making it.

Allen suddenly gestured, catching her attention. There was a break in the granite, a natural alcove. It was their best chance for survival. The winds had picked up and the fire was moving faster now. They were out of options.

Elaine ordered her crew under their fire blankets as she radioed their coordinates. The second drop she had called for had been delayed due to the high winds but was en route and would change course to provide them support.

Everyone scrambled under their blankets, using the granite to their advantage to shield themselves as the fire bore down on them. She lay under her shield feeling the temperature rise as the flames rolled over them seeking fuel on the other side of their hold. She could feel a blister forming under her heavy glove and hoped it was the only one.

It would be so easy to give in to the beast. Elaine closed her eyes against the pain searing through her body. The pain told her to run, to get away, anywhere was better than here. Only her mind kept her where she was. There was no place safe to run to. She closed her eyes and for the first time since leaving the bus let herself think about Devon. She could see herself years from now with Devon by her side. She would endure any pain to get back to the woman she loved. The truth of her words echoed in her mind; *a lifetime with Devon wouldn't be long enough.*

The roaring was not as loud now and the temperature had dropped slightly. The rocks had protected them as the fire rolled over the crew. She hadn't heard the plane that had dropped chemical suppressant intended to extinguish the flames, but when she pulled back her blanket, she was relieved to see everything covered in red.

It was a beautiful sight.

Behind the flames there was a strange calm. They took stock of their injuries, raising their masks so they could talk. Tom's glove had failed and his hand was damn near blistered to the bone. The best she could offer the distressed man was a quick field dressing. She smiled at him, trying to take his mind off the pain. "Your wife is going to skin me for this."

Tom grimaced. "Yeah, well you don't have to live with her."

Elaine laughed. "I'll tell her you said that."

"Oh, come on Cap, why do you have to be that way?"

Elaine smiled. "Because I love you, that's why."

"Come on, let's get you up." Brad helped Elaine get Tom on his feet. As the shock wore off, the pain would be relentless and he didn't have time to surrender to it. They had a lot of ground to cover before they could get him the medical attention he so badly needed.

Elaine quickly gathered her team, which now included a couple of the firefighters they had rescued and they once again made their way across the ridge.

The sun was rising when they finally met up with another crew, also waiting for transit out. She found a place to sit, her back to a rock and didn't remember anything more.

It was noon before she found medical attention and rations for her men and herself. Elaine was exhausted and she just wanted to crawl into the back of a truck and crash for the rest of the day. Sleep invited her, but calling Devon was more important. She had to nurse her battery for all it was worth—recharge stations were a luxury. Just dialing the number took what little energy she had remaining, but she absolutely had to hear Devon's voice. She needed her comfort.

"Hi."

"Oh God, Elaine, you sound terrible."

"I'm fine. I just wanted to hear your voice before I go to sleep again."

Elaine could hear the tension in Devon's voice. "You're okay, right? You're safe?"

"I'm safe." It was the truth, even if not the whole truth.

"You need to rest."

"I miss you, Devon."

"I think it goes without saying that I miss you too."

"How are you holding up?"

The line crackled. "Don't worry about me. Just come back to

me in one piece. How long will you be out there?"

"I don't know. At least a couple of weeks. Now we plan for the runoff when it rains, try to direct the ash where it'll do the least amount of damage. Lots of digging."

"Sooner or later someone like me will make sure you did a good job."

She could tell Devon was trying to cheer her, but she couldn't hold off sleep any longer. "I'll be home soon. I love you."

Devon's voice was soft. "I love you, too. Sweet dreams."

Chapter 22

Devon arrived at the station parking lot, frazzled and worried. In the three weeks since Elaine had left she'd become worried that Elaine was hurt and not telling her. It was irrational, but short sporadic phone calls weren't reassuring, though she was profoundly grateful for them. She needed to see for herself that Elaine was all right. She wouldn't be able to breathe again until Elaine was in her arms.

Elaine's truck was there, looking like it had been driven to hell and back.

Devon passed several doors before a nice looking gentleman, who looked like he was in desperate need of sleep, stepped out of his office. "May I help you?"

"I'm looking for Captain Elaine Thomas. The woman at the front desk said that she was over this way somewhere."

He held out his hand and flashed a warm smile.

"Hi, I'm Brad. If I see the Cap, can I tell her who is looking for her?"

Devon smiled at his welcoming charm and because she recognized him as one of Elaine's crew members. Elaine thought very highly of her men. That meant she did too. "Devon McKinney."

Brad's smile grew as if hearing her name was the best news he had heard all day.

"You might try looking just down the hall. She may be outside." He pointed to glass doors leading outside. "That's where the smokers go for a break."

Devon gave him a puzzled look. Elaine didn't smoke, but he acted as if he knew what he was talking about so she followed his directions. As she was about to pass through the doors, Devon came to a dead stop.

Elaine stood talking to an attractive woman who was stroking her arm affectionately. At first, all Devon could see was her lover. Exhaustion was etched across her face and she looked like she hadn't had a decent shower since she'd left. She was thinner and looked as though she was in desperate need of a good meal. Devon almost pushed through the door, but Elaine's distant expression made Devon take a second look at the other woman. Perhaps they were just colleagues.

But when someone opened the door to come back in, Devon was able to catch part of their conversation. The woman laughed and spoke coyly, "I'm glad you're back, darling, it felt like you were gone forever."

Elaine pulled her arm away from the other woman's touch. Before the doors closed Elaine answered, "Grace, I doubt very much that you even noticed I was gone."

Grace! This woman who was touching Elaine, this woman hanging on Elaine, this was Grace? She was an extremely attractive woman and flaunted it almost like a weapon.

After everything Elaine had told her about Grace, seeing the viper for real still stunned her. The gall! Devon was torn between marching out there and ripping this woman's head off for the pain she had put Elaine through and standing right here so she could watch Elaine do it.

She had been gone for weeks and Devon knew she would be tired and sore and a confrontation with Grace was the last thing she needed now.

She knew she shouldn't eavesdrop, but she doubted any woman in the world could have walked away at that moment. She stood against the wall out of the way of those passing by, but still in plain sight should either of them glance her way and close enough that she was still able to hear what was being said.

Why Grace had insisted they step outside was beyond Elaine. But rather than allowing Grace to make a scene, she had agreed. She was tired and wanted nothing more than to go home to Devon's waiting arms. She ached to see her lover.

She was too tired to deal with Grace, but it was easier to listen to her now than fight with her later. Grace had been one of the few rangers to stay behind to manage their own state from within the safe confines of the ranger station. It was so like Grace to volunteer for *that* duty.

She crossed her arms across her chest as Grace prattled about unimportant things, not really wanting to hear anything that Grace had to say.

Elaine wasn't buying her I-was-worried-about-you-because-I-care act for a moment. "I don't know what was so important that you had to drag me out here, but I doubt that you have anything to say that I would be interested in hearing unless it's station business."

Grace made a motion with her hand as if she were waving Elaine's words aside. It was a gesture that Elaine knew too well and hated. "Come on, Laney, don't be that way."

Grace's voice was practically a whine and Elaine's patience was wearing thin. Everything they had once shared had been over a long time ago and was washed away all those weeks ago in the stream.

The thought of that stream brought a slight smile to her lips. That was the day she had met Devon and her life began. She couldn't wait to get out of here. She had a few days off and she intended to spend them getting reacquainted with the woman she so desperately loved.

Grace's laughter interrupted her thoughts. "Oh Elaine, I do love you."

Elaine ignored the people who were finishing their break. It was obvious they were trying to be discreet about leaving the area and the private conversation they couldn't help but overhear. "I loved you too, Grace. Past tense." She was grateful when the door closed again. "At least I thought I loved you. Now I don't know you. You were an important part of my life. But now I can see that we haven't loved each other in a very long time. I loved the idea of what we *could be*. But we both know that the fantasy ended long before your affair."

Grace leaned in to kiss her as though that would change Elaine's mind. As soon as she realized Grace's intention, Elaine was overwhelmed by revulsion. These lips had lied to her and cheated on her. These lips weren't Devon's.

She pushed her away. "I don't know what kind of game you are trying to play, but I want no part of it. Don't you dare touch me again."

Grace regained her composure quickly and interrupted Elaine. "It's no game, darling. Don't you see? I had to be with someone else…for us."

Her jaw dropped as Grace continued. "I had to sleep with someone else to remind us both of what we had been missing. That's why I brought you out here, to tell you that I'm ready for us to be together again. Don't you remember how good we were together?"

Elaine remembered the betrayal. She remembered Grace's biting words and the cold, calculated way she had learned that

Grace was moving in with someone else. She remembered how invisible she felt when she was with Grace. So different from how alive and comfortable and loved and safe she felt with Devon.

With a firm steady voice, so that Grace—and anyone else in earshot—could not misconstrue her words, Elaine said, "I'm sorry, Grace, but I don't want you back. I don't love you. I deserve better than you and I always did. I don't want to live in the past and I don't want to live with someone I don't trust. Most importantly, I don't want to live with someone that I no longer like. I don't want to hurt you and I don't want you to think I harbor any ill will toward you, but I can honestly say that I feel nothing for you and I have no desire to be your leftovers, not now, not ever again. Can I possibly be any clearer? Don't bring this subject up again and don't drag me out here in full view of our colleagues like this again. I won't tolerate it."

Elaine paused, making sure her words were sinking in. "Your walking out was the best thing that could have ever happened to me. I now know what true love is and I have found that with someone else. I've moved on, Grace. I certainly hope that you can too."

Without another word, Elaine spun on her heel. She was done.

Then she saw Devon. Beautiful, strong, tender and nothing but a thin pane of glass separated them. Their eyes locked and it seemed like it had been forever since she had touched her and kissed her. She flung open the door hardly able to contain an intimate embrace.

"I'm so proud of you baby," Devon whispered with a warm loving smile on her face. It was clear that Devon had heard every word that Elaine had said. Elaine's eyes swept over the short skirt and tailored blouse. Her mouth went dry as it always did when she saw Devon, no matter what she was or wasn't wearing.

"It was just the truth—" Before she could finish her sentence, someone seized her shoulder and spun her around.

Grace was seething and Elaine thought irrelevantly that it

was really quite unattractive. "Don't think that I buy for one second that you really found another woman, darling. You were damn lucky to have me and don't think any *lady* will be as tolerant of you as I was…always coming home covered in filth." Grace huffed childishly.

She realized she was just too tired to deal when Devon stepped around her into view.

Grace's expression instantly changed. She wore a sickening sugary smile as she looked Devon up and down.

Devon's voice resembled that of someone who was giving a stranger directions but Elaine could see the disdain Devon felt for Grace burning in her eyes. "You must be Grace."

Grace pulled herself up and offered her hand. "Yes and you would be?"

Devon looked down at the proffered hand with contempt, then locked gazes with Grace. "My name is *Doctor* Devon McKinney. The *lady* who is lucky enough to share Elaine's bed every night and who has eagerly looked forward to her return."

Devon pulled Elaine to her side and it seemed totally natural to give her a kiss, but the instant their lips met, the kiss stopped being for Grace's benefit and instantly became about them. She felt Devon's joyful response, forgot about Grace and that they were at the ranger station. All that mattered was that they were in each other's arms again. Elaine was safe and home and their long separation was over. It wasn't until Brad discreetly cleared his throat behind them that they parted breathless and several more seconds before they broke eye contact.

"Let's get out of here," Elaine managed to say.

Devon got that look in her eye, the same look as when she started a snowball fight. She gave Grace a sideways glance. "I really should thank you. If you hadn't been foolish enough to give up such a wonderful woman, I might never have known the wonder of loving her and being loved by her."

As they began to turn away, Devon paused. "Oh and Grace?" She waited for Grace to make eye contact before smiling sweetly at her. "Smart ladies love to have their women come home filthy, because it's so *very* enjoyable helping them get *all* clean."

Elaine heard snickers from the onlookers, who had all been trying to look as if they weren't listening in. Grace had asked for it and if Elaine hadn't already been planning to kiss Devon, she would have just for that.

Elaine couldn't get the silly grin off her face. She knew she was in for some good-natured ribbing from her guys later, but even that was perfectly okay. "I need something from my office. It's over here."

Elaine led them into her office and closed the office door behind them, leaning against it for a moment.

Devon turned and looked at the floor before raising her eyes to Elaine's. "I'm sorry about that." She waved her hand in the direction they had just come from.

"You are?" Elaine took a step toward her.

Devon bit her lower lip in the way she did when she was nervous about something. A habit that Elaine found endearing. "Well, not about what I said to Grace."

"So you aren't?" Another step.

Devon shook her head. "Not unless I said something that hurt you."

Elaine smiled. "You didn't say anything that wasn't true." Another step.

Devon looked her square in the eyes. "I wanted to kiss you. I needed to kiss you."

Elaine's smile grew. "To make a point?" She was just a step away from Devon now.

"At first…yes. But you know that when it comes to kissing you I can't stop at just a peck. Once I touch your lips I can't stop and…Oh God, Elaine, I'm so sorry if I embarrassed you or got you into any kind of trouble."

Elaine pulled Devon into her arms. "Right now every man and lesbian out there wishes they were me." Elaine gave her a crooked smile. "Hell, I think half the straight women wish they were too. You are a beautiful and amazing woman and I am so incredibly in love with you, *Doctor* Devon McKinney."

"I'm so completely in love with you too Captain Thomas." Devon smiled sheepishly and bit her lip again. "So how much trouble will you be in?"

Elaine looked steadily into Devon's eyes so she could see the truth there. "None. And even if I were I would gladly accept it. Grace is the one who brought our personal life into the workplace and she will be the one who deals with the consequences. I'm done paying for her mistakes."

"Enough about her, then." Devon slid her hand into Elaine's ash-covered hair and pulled her in for a soulful kiss. When they pulled apart to breathe Devon whispered, "I've been dreaming about that every single night since you left."

"Devon, if I didn't need a shower so bad I would make love to you right here on my desk."

Devon smiled and ran her finger along Elaine's bottom lip. "As tempting as that sounds, I wasn't lying about what I told Grace out there. One of my favorite things about your job is how much I love helping you get clean after a hard day's work."

Elaine felt her knees weaken.

"Can you come home now or do you have to stay longer?"

"I have some reports that need to be filed, but I can submit them online. And since I've been gone for so long I have a few days off. What about you?"

"To keep myself from going crazy worrying about you, I worked...*a lot*. So I arranged to have a few days off."

Elaine smiled. "You did, huh?"

"Yep, I figured since you were busy saving our forests you might need a little pampering when you got home."

The prospect of being in Devon's arms, making love, sleeping and waking up to do it all over again seemed to make her feel not so tired after all. "What did you have in mind?"

Devon hooked her arm around Elaine's. "Why don't you grab your gear and I'll take you home and show you. We might even find the time to call for delivery to keep your strength up."

"Oh God, woman!"

Devon leaned forward and purred in Elaine's ear, "You can leave your truck here. I'll bring you back to get it in a few days."

"A few days?"

"You won't need it before then."

"I won't?"

Devon smiled. "I'm still debating about whether I'm actually going to let you out of bed over the next few days."

Elaine swallowed and suddenly couldn't get the office door open fast enough. "Lead the way, my love. I'll gladly follow you anywhere."

Heads turned at Devon's laughter.

Someone called, "Heading out, Cap?"

"I'm going home," she answered as she slipped her arm around her lover's waist and they walked out into the sunshine together.

**Publications from
Bella Books, Inc.**
Women. Books. Even Better Together.

**P.O. Box 10543
Tallahassee, FL 32302
Phone: 800-729-4992
www.bellabooks.com**

THE GRASS WIDOW by Nanci Little. Aidan Blackstone is nineteen, unmarried and pregnant and has no reason to think that the year 1876 won't be her last. Joss Bodett has lost her family but desperately clings to their land. A richly told story of frontier survival that picks up with the generation of women where Patience and Sarah left off.
978-1-59493-189-5 $12.95

SMOKEY O by Celia Cohen. Insult "Mac" MacDonnell and insult the entire Delaware Blue Diamond team. Smokey O'Neill has just insulted Mac and then finds she's been traded to Delaware. The games are not limited to the baseball field!
978-1-59493-198-7 $12.95

WICKED GAMES by Ellen Hart. Never have mysteries and secrets been closer to home in this eighth installment of this award-winning lesbian cozy mystery series. Jane Lawless's neighbors bring puzzles and peril—and that's just the beginning.
978-1-59493-185-7 $14.95

NOT EVERY RIVER by Robbi McCoy. It's the hottest city in the U.S. and it's not just the weather that's heating up. For Kim and Randi are forced to question everything they thought they knew about themselves before they can risk their fiery hearts on the biggest gamble of all.
978-1-59493-182-6 $14.95

HOUSE OF CARDS by Nat Burns. Cards are played, but the game is gossip. Kaylen Strauder has never wanted it to be about her. But the time is fast-approaching when she must decide which she needs more: her community or Eda Byrne.
978-1-59493-203-8 $14.95

RETURN TO ISIS by Jean Stewart. The award-winning Isis sci-fi series features Jean Stewart's vision of a committed colony of women dedicated to preserving their way of life, even after the apocalypse. Mysteries have been forgotten, but survival depends on remembering. Book one in series.
978-1-59493-193-2 $12.95

1ST IMPRESSIONS by Kate Calloway. Rookie PI Cassidy James has her first case. Her investigation into the murder of Erica Trinidad's uncle isn't welcomed by the local sheriff, especially since the delicious, seductive Erica is their prime suspect. first in series. Author's augmented and expanded edition.
978-1-59493-192-5 $12.95

BEACON OF LOVE by Ann Roberts. Twenty-five years after their families put an end to a relationship that hadn't even begun, Stephanie returns to Oregon to find many things have changed...except her feelings for Paula.
978-1-59493-180-2 $14.95

ABOVE TEMPTATION by Karin Kallmaker. It's supposed to be like any other case, except this time they're chasing one of their own. As fraud investigators Tamara Sterling and Kip Barrett try to catch a thief, they realize they can have anything they want—except each other.
978-1-59493-179-6 $14.95

AN EMERGENCE OF GREEN by Katherine V. Forrest. Carolyn had no idea her new neighbor jumped the fence to enjoy her swimming pool. The discovery leads to choices she never anticipated in an intense, sensual story of discovery and risk, consequences and triumph. Originally released in 1986.
978-1-59493-217-5 $14.95

CRAZY FOR LOVING by Jaye Maiman. Officially hanging out her shingle as a private investigator, Robin Miller is getting her life on track. Just as Robin discovers it's hard to follow a dead man, she walks in. KT Bellflower, sultry and devastating... Lammy winner and second in series.
978-1-59493-195-6 $14.95

LOVE WAITS by Gerri Hill. The All-American girl and the love she left behind—it's been twenty years since Ashleigh and Gina parted and now they're back to the place where nothing was simple and love didn't wait.
978-1-59493-186-4 $14.95

HANNAH FREE: THE BOOK by Claudia Allen. Based on the film festival hit movie starring Sharon Gless. Hannah's story is funny, scathing and witty as she navigates life with aplomb—but always comes home to Rachel. 32 pages of color photographs plus bonus behind-the-scenes movie information.
978-1-59493-172-7 $19.95

END OF THE ROPE by Jackie Calhoun. Meg Klein has two enduring loves—horses and Nicky Hennessey. Nicky is there for her when she most needs help, but then an attractive vet throws Meg's carefully balanced world out of kilter.
978-1-59493-176-5 $14.95

THE LONG TRAIL by Penny Hayes. When schoolteacher Blanche Bartholomew and dance hall girl Teresa Stark meet their feelings are powerful—and completely forbidden—in Starcross Texas. In search of a safe future, they flee, daring to take a covered wagon across the forbidding prairie.
978-1-59493-196-3 $12.95

UP UP AND AWAY by Catherine Ennis. Sarah and Margaret have a video. The mob wants it. Flying for their lives, two women discover more than secrets.
978-1-59493-215-1 $12.95

CITY OF STRANGERS by Diana Rivers. A captive in a gilded cage, young Solene plots her escape, but the rulers of Hernorium have other plans for Solene—and her people. Breathless lesbian fantasy story also perfect for teen readers.
978-1-59493-183-3 $14.95

ROBBER'S WINE by Ellen Hart. Belle Dumont is the first dead of summer. Jane Lawless, Belle's old friend, suspects coldhearted murder. Lammy-winning seventh novel in critically acclaimed cozy mystery series.
978-1-59493-184-0 $14.95

APPARITION ALLEY by Katherine V. Forrest. Kate Delafield has solved hundreds of cases, but the one that baffles her most is her own shooting. Book six in series.
978-1-883523-65-7 $14.95

STERLING ROAD BLUES by Ruth Perkinson. It was a simple declaration of love. But the entire state of Virginia wants to weigh in, leaving teachers Carrie Tomlinson and Audra Malone caught in the crossfire—and with love troubles of their own.
978-1-59493-187-1 $14.95

LILY OF THE TOWER by Elizabeth Hart. Agnes Headey, taking refuge from a storm at the Netherfield estate, stumbles into dark family secrets and something more...Meticulously researched historical romance.
978-1-59493-177-2 $14.95

LETTING GO by Ann O'Leary. Kelly has decided that luscious, successful Laura should be hers. For now. Laura might even be agreeable. But where does that leave Kate?
978-1-59493-194-9 $12.95

MURDER TAKES TO THE HILLS by Jessica Thomas. Renovations, shady business deals, a stalker—and it's not even tourist season yet for PI Alex Peres and her best four-legged pal Fargo. Sixth in this cozy Provincetown-based series.
978-1-59493-178-9 $14.95